{ *The Back* Room *by* **Carmen** **Martín** *Gaite*

Translated from the Spanish by Helen Lane

City Lights Books
San Francisco

First published as *El cuarto de atrás* © 1978 Carmen Martín Gaite and
Ediciones Destino, S.L.

Book design: Elaine Katzenberger
Cover design: Rex Ray
Typography: Harvest Graphics

Library of Congress Cataloging in Publication Data

Martín Gaite, Carmen.
    [Cuarto de atrás. English]
    The back room / by Carmen Martín Gaite ; translated from the
Spanish by Helen Lane.
       p. cm.
    ISBN 0-87286-371-9
    I. Lane, Helen R. II. Title.
    PQ6623.A7657 C8132000
    863'.64—dc21   99-088257

City Lights Books are available to bookstores through our primary
distributor: Subterranean Company, P.O. Box 160, 265 S. 5th St.,
Monroe, OR 97456. 541-847-5274. FAX 541-847-6018. Our books
are also available through library jobbers and regional distributors.
For personal orders and catalogs, please write to City Lights Books,
261 Columbus Avenue, San Francisco, CA 94133. Visit our web site:
www.citylights.com

CITY LIGHTS BOOKS are edited by Lawrence Ferlinghetti and
Nancy J. Peters and published at the City Lights Bookstore,
261 Columbus Avenue, San Francisco, CA 94133.

For Lewis Carroll, who still consoles us for being so sensible
and welcomes us into his world turned topsy-turvy

CONTENTS

"Experience cannot be communicated without bonds of silence, concealment, distance." —Georges Bataille

THE bAREfOOT MAN

. . . AND YET I'D swear that the position was the same—I think I've always slept this way, with my right arm underneath the pillow and my body turned slightly over onto that side, my feet searching for the place where the sheet is tucked in. What's more, if I close my eyes—and I end up closing them as a last, routine resort—I am visited by a long-familiar apparition, always the same: a parade of stars, each with a clown's face, that go soaring up like a balloon that's escaped and laugh with a frozen grin, following one after the other in a zigzag pattern, like spirals of smoke gradually becoming thicker and thicker. There are so many of them that in a little while there won't be any room left for them and they'll have to descend to seek more space in the riverbed of my blood, and then they'll be petals that the river carries away. At the moment they're rising in bunches. I see the minuscule face drawn in the center of each one of them, like a cherry pit surrounded by spangles. But what never changes is the tune that accompanies the ascent, a melody that can't be heard yet marks the beat, a special silence whose very denseness makes it count more than it would if it could be heard. This was the most typical thing back then too. I recognized that strange silence as being the prelude to something that was about to happen. I breathed slowly, I felt my insides pulsing, my ears buzzing, and my blood locked in. At any moment—where exactly?—that ascending multitude would fall and swell the invisible inner flow like an intravenous drug, capable of altering all my visions. And I was wide awake, awaiting the prodigious change, so lightning-quick that there was never a night when I managed to trap the very instant of its sudden stealthy appearance as I lay in wait there, watching for it eagerly and fearfully, just as I'm doing now.

But that's not true, it wasn't just the same, the exact feel of the waiting was different. I have said "eagerly and fearfully," just to hear myself talk, groping my way along blindly, and when one takes a shot at random that way, one never hits the bull's-eye. Words are for the light. At night they run away, though the heat of the chase is more feverish and compelling in the dark, but for that very reason it is also a more fruitless one. Trying at one and the same time to understand and to dream: that is the fate to which my nights are doomed. Back then, I wasn't trying to understand anything. I saw the swarm of stars rising, heard the ringing of the silence, and felt the touch of the sheet. I hugged the pillow and lay there quietly, but how could it possibly be the same now! I awaited the transformation submerged in a pleasurable impatience, like just before going in to the circus, when my parents were getting the tickets, and would say to me: "Don't get lost in all this confusion." And I would stand there quietly, amid the confusion, staring fascinated at the posters showing what I was about to see in just a little while—a bit afraid, of course, because the lions might look at me or the trapeze artist might fall from the very top of the tent, but also ready, willing, and eager, and above all enjoying that wait, experiencing it knowing that the best part is always the waiting; I've believed that ever since I was a little girl, up until quite recently. I'd give anything to relive that sensation, sell my soul to the Devil just to experience it again, if only for a few minutes; I might understand the ways in which it differs from this irritation out of the midst of which I am trying to summon it now, a vain summons. The words dance and move farther and farther away from me, it's like being bent on reading small print without one's glasses.

So what shall I do? . . . I'm helpless without my glasses, I'll busy myself making simple drawings, that will rest my eyes; I'm going to imagine that I'm drawing lines in the sand of the beach with a little stick. It's lots of fun because the sand is hard and the little stick is sharp, or maybe it's a sharp-pointed seashell, it doesn't matter. I don't know what beach it is either, it might be Zumaya or La Lanzada, it's late in the afternoon and there isn't anybody around, the sun is going down, red and flattened in the haze, to take a dip in the sea. I'm painting, I'm painting, what am I painting? What color am I using and what letter? The *C* of my name, three things beginning with *C*, a *casa* first, then a *cuarto,* and then a *cama.**** The apartment has an old-fashioned balcony overlooking a little square. You

*House, bedroom, bed. (*Translator's note.*)

paint the thick parallel bars of the railing and behind them the doors leading inside, left open because it was spring, and from the little square (though I don't paint it, I see it, I see it again every time) there came the sound of water splashing through three pipes into the basin of a fountain that stood in the middle, the only sound to be heard in the bedroom at night. We've gotten as far as the bedroom now: you begin at the corner of the ceiling, and running down from there, the vertical line where the walls come together. There we are. There's no need to draw the line all the way down to the floor because the bed, a studio couch against the wall in the corner, is hiding it. In the daytime there were cushions on it and you could stretch out on it when you were bored. It's easy to paint: a simple rectangle, without a headboard, the two slightly curved lines of the pillow, the vertical line of the sheet folded back and the rest of the space filled with little wavy tildes like those over *ñ*'s, representing the design on the spread. And that's all. It hasn't turned out very well, but it doesn't matter. It can be completed by closing your eyes. To do that it's best to keep them closed: changing the décor has always been the specialty of the little flashing stars, the first number of the performance they're announcing up there in the air with their clown's laugh.

The shifting back and forth has started, I no longer can tell if I'm lying in this bed or in that one. I think, rather, that I'm moving from one to the other. At certain times what predominates is the layout — as natural to me as a second skin — of the furniture whose presence I could substantiate merely by stretching out my arm and turning the light on. But then, with no transition, that drawing that insinuated itself onto the sand of the beach superimposes itself, and this big bed surrounded by books and papers in which I was seeking consolation a little while ago vanishes, displaced by the one in the bedroom off the balcony, and I begin to perceive the feel of the bedspread, a rough fabric in blue tones. That fabric had a name, I don't remember what it was, all fabrics had one, and it was essential to know how to tell a shantung from a piqué, a moiré, or an organdy. Not to be able to recognize fabrics by their names was as scandalous as to call neighbors by the wrong names. There were many drygoods shops, long and dark, many sorts of fabrics, and as one stood in front of the counter one signaled with a knowledgeable gesture to the clerk, who was always most deferent, to take the bolt of material that had been pointed to over to the door and unroll it in order to display its outstanding virtues in the light. One never bought anything at first sight, one consulted with one's women friends or one's husband: "I saw some very pretty material for the girls' room." My mother copied the idea of how to decorate that room from the magazine *Lecturas* and sewed the curtains herself, with matching flounced bedspreads and pillow covers with a sort of sash that fastened around the middle of them, and then the cushions—of different material but in the same color—which—on being thrown on the couch in a studied disorder, completed the daily transformation of that décor. The little round lamps in yellow glass, the knickknacks on the shelves, the night tables lacquered in blue: it was all very modern—art deco as it's called nowadays—but what seemed most modern to me was the fact that the bed could be converted into a couch and I could stretch out on it when I was alone, imitating the attitude of those women, so remote as to be nonexistent, who appeared in the illustrations drawn by Emilio Freixas in *Lecturas* for the novelettes by Elisabeth Mulder, whom I envied because of her name and because she wrote novelettes, women with dreamy eyes, hair cut in a "boyish bob," and stylized legs, who had conversations on the telephone, held a tall glass between their fingers, or smoked Turkish cigarettes on the "Turkish bed" of their *garçonnière* (if anything was "Turkish" it was "modern"). At other times they appeared in lounge pajamas with wide floppy legs, but even though it was nighttime they were always awake, waiting for something, most likely a telephone call, and behind their bitter lips and their half-closed eyes lay hidden the secret story that they were recollecting in solitude.

When it took me a long time to drop off to sleep—I always took longer than my sister—and the stars began to rise inside my eyelids like spirals of smoke from Turkish cigarettes, the room changed into another one. There was a telephone, but not the black telephone hanging on the wall opposite the bench in the hallway, on which messages were received for my father, or the occasional call from a schoolmate of mine at the Institute, a girl with slightly bulging eyes who had a terrible time taking notes in class ("Is this 1438? . . . Hey listen, this is Toñi"). No, this phone sat on top of the night table, within reach of my hand, and it was white: a white telephone, the quintessence of the unattainable. Moreover, the bedroom belonged to me alone, and if I turned on the light I didn't bother anybody. It was a room on the top floor of a skyscraper. I could turn the light on, get up out of bed, take a bath at midnight, rub my body with beauty products from the House of Gal, read a letter that I had received that afternoon in which someone contemplating the sea said that he was thinking of me, put on a chiffon dress, take the elevator downstairs and step out into a city full of bright lights, wander aimlessly about amid passersby who cast sidelong glances at me, avoid the risk of our eyes meeting, enter a café called the Negresco with a resolute tapping of my high heels and evasive gestures, allow my absent gaze to wander over the black marble tabletops, the Cubist surfaces and the mirrors wreathed in smoke, light a Turkish cigarette, wait.

I crept out of bed on tiptoe so as not to wake my sister up and went out onto the balcony. It was a second floor apartment. I saw the shadow of the trees just beyond, and across the street the façade of the Iglesia del Carmen with its bell tower. The only sound to be heard was the water falling into the basin of the fountain. The street lamps shed a faint glow. Not a soul was passing by, perhaps I was the only person awake beneath the stars that were keeping watch over the city as it slept. I looked at them for a long time, as though to fill up the storehouse in my eyelids. Cold little pinheads. I smiled with my eyes closed, I liked feeling the cool night air stealing through my nightdress: "Some day I'll have sorrows to weep over, stories to remember, wide avenues to wander down. I'll be able to leave the house and lose myself in the night." The lava of my bouts of insomnia was seething with the future.

It's no use, I can't get to sleep. I've turned on the light, the hands of the clock have stopped at ten. It seems to me that

that was what time it was when I climbed into bed, intending to take notes. The dial of the clock has the mysterious glow of a dead moon. I sit up in bed and the room tilts like a landscape seen from a plane pitching forward: the books, the piles of clothes on the armchair, the night table, the pictures on the wall, everything is tilted. I thrust my feet out of the bed and contemplate them in amazement, they look like two handfuls of goose barnacles on the inclined plane of the gray carpet. When I stand up I'm surely going to fall, and it may very well be that the weight of my body will cause the floor to sway back and forth even more violently and the room to pivot and turn upside down. I hope so, I'm going to try, it must be amusing to walk around upside down.

I rise to my feet and the swing rights itself, as do the ceiling, the walls, and the long rectangular frame of the mirror in front of which I stand motionless, disappointed. The room reflected in its quicksilvered depths seems unreal to me in its static reality. Behind my back everything is right side up again, perfectly in plumb, and I am so taken aback by the gaze of that vertical figure, with its arms dangling down the sides of its blue pajamas, beaming back at me from the mirror, that it scares me. I whirl about anxiously, wanting to recapture the truth in that dislocation glimpsed a few seconds before by taking it by surprise, but outside the mirror the normality that it has reflected persists, and perhaps for this very reason the disorder that reigns there is even more depressingly obvious: shoes on the floor, a cushion that has fallen, magazines, and looking down at me from all the shelves and horizontal surfaces, lying in ambush like stuffed animals, that jumble of objects whose history, embedded in their silhouettes, awakens muffled echoes in my memory and scrapes unsuspected depths in my soul, dredging up dates, rotten fruits. What a hodgepodge of posters, photographs, odds and ends, books . . . ! Books that, to make things even messier, have dates, slips of paper, telegrams, drawings inside them, one text on top of another—dozens of books that I could merely open and then close again, whereupon they would immediately be out of place, piled one atop the other, proliferating like weeds. A lady I know, may she rest in peace, who spent her life fighting against the anarchy of objects, used to say that the minute you leave a book on top of a radiator, it instantly gives birth to another. I walk over to the radiator. I really should get busy and tidy up this room. I stop and look at it from here. The bed is now enormous, if it grew any bigger it would drive me into the corner and crush me, but no, it doesn't get any bigger, a strip of carpet still separates me from its bottom edge. I wonder what it was I came over here to look for, if in fact I was looking for something, perhaps a pill to put me to sleep—Mogadon, Pelson, Dapaz—or to wake me up—Dexedrine, Maxibamato—or to get rid of a headache—Cafiaspirina, Optalidón, Fiorinal. Those are names that come to my mind automatically, names that it bores me to run through, that I've lost all faith in, names as over-familiar as those in my list of phone numbers, friends I've lost all desire to call upon for anything.

Above the radiator is a set of knickknack shelves lacquered in white with lathe-turned bars at each end—an *étagère*, as they used to be called in the years of art deco—and in a gap between two groups of books, pinned to the wall with thumb-tacks, is a black and white print approximately eight inches high and five inches wide. It has been there across from my bed for a long time now, and in the middle of certain long sleepless nights, when the real and the fictitious become confused, the thought has occurred to me that it was a little mirror reflecting, with a slight distortion, the very situation that had led me to look over at it. It shows a man with very dark hair and eyes who is leaning on his left elbow in a bed with a canopy. His nightshirt is unbuttoned and the shadow of his torso is projected onto the circular curtains that fall in folds from the tall flounce edged with fringe overhead. His two hands are outside the sheet. He is resting his head on one of them and in a gesture that appears to be meant to emphasize words that cannot be heard, the index finger of his other hand is pointing toward the second figure in the print. This figure is naked, and with the exception of the corneas of his two eyes, is totally black. The skin on his body is black, his curly hair is black, his pointed ears are black, his horns are black, the two huge wings on his back are black. He is shown in profile, sitting on a table loaded with books, with his feet resting on another pile of books that are lying on the floor, and from there—leaning his elbows on his knees and holding his chin between his two fists that are touching at the wrists—he is insolently meeting the somber and penetrating gaze of the person speaking to him. The legend underneath reads: "Luther's Discussion with the Devil," and it helps me to escape from the spell that the room in the print was beginning to cast over me. It seemed to me that it was taking on depth and relief, that I was entering it, and lowering my eyes to the title has been like coming out of it, before the lips of the figures began to move or the unstable equilibrium of the books on which the Devil is carelessly resting his heels was shattered. Legends orient us, help us to escape from abysses and labyrinths, but the nostalgia of the perdition that was imminent nonetheless lingers on.

I look farther downward. More books, forming two walls above the radiator, and between them, holding them in place, the sewing basket that belonged to Grandma Rosario. It is stuffed so full it almost won't shut. I am unable to fathom how so many things can fit inside it. I always look in it first thing whenever I'm perplexed. Everything inevitably ends up there inside it. It's a foregone conclusion that when I open it I'll remember what I was in the midst of searching for. I tug on one of its handles, the walls of books that it was holding in place lose their support and a number of them tumble down in a spectacular cascade. Just as I am about to bend over to pick them up, with the sewing basket in my hand, I slip on one of them and I too tumble to the floor. From the half-open wicker lid there come spilling out spools of thread, electric plugs, cubes of sugar, thimbles, safety pins, bills, a candle end, snapshots, buttons, coins, bottles of pills, everything imaginable, all tangled up in colored thread.

I haven't hurt myself. I reach for a pillow, place it between my back and the bottom edge of the bed and sit there in the narrow strip of hallway, contemplating the objects scattered all about and the threads tying together their heterogeneous profiles. Over there is the book that made me lose my footing: *Introduction to Fantastic Literature,* * by Todorov. Well it's about time, I've been hunting for it for I don't know how long. It deals with the subject of split personalities, of breaking through the boundaries between time and space, of ambiguity and uncertainty. It's one of those books that wake you up and set you to taking notes furiously. When I finished it, I wrote in a notebook: "I swear I'm going to write a fantastic novel." I suppose it was a promise I made to Todorov. That was around the middle of January, five months have gone by since then. Projects often flare up like will-o'-the-wisps in the heat of certain readings, but then when one's enthusiasm flags it's of little use to return to the source that aroused it, because what's missing, as usual, is the incandescent spark of the first encounter. The covers of the book, which is lying alongside a gold thimble, begin to fade. The light flickers and grows dimmer, it's comfortable sitting here on the floor; I relive my pleasure of long ago at lingering about in passageways, odd corners, attics, that childish predilection for hiding-places. "They won't find me here," that was the first thought that used to come to mind as I settled down to feed my fantasies. I can play now too. The objects scattered all about look like fetishes, the pieces of furniture are the tops of trees, I'm lost in the woods, amid treasures that I alone discover. Something is going to happen to me, the secret is to wait without becoming anxious, to let oneself drift. We've lost our love of playing

---

*As published in English: *The Fantastic: A Structural Approach to a Literary Genre,* tr. from the French by R. Howard (Ithaca: Cornell University Press, 1975)—*ed.*

games just for the fun of it, and basically it's so easy. I'm going to make myself more comfortable.

I give Todorov a push with my foot. That fall of mine was right out of a Buster Keaton movie. How those calamities of silent films, that later on I myself played the leading role in a thousand times over, used to make me laugh: falling out of a chair, tumbling down stairs, breaking dishes, spattering pie all over a new dress, getting singed in fires one has lighted oneself, repeated accidents which, each time they happen yet again, relieve the tension and restore one's sense of identity as no deliberate effort can, clumsy acts revealing the insecurity of the antihero.

The sewing basket is still lying alongside me, a vessel that has come through the shipwreck with a handful of survivors in the hold. I place it in my lap and beneath an amber-colored buckle I discover a folded sheet of paper glowing with a strange phosphorescence. I take it out of the basket and begin unfolding it. It has so many folds in it that as I spread it out, it gradually turns into a larger and larger surface. I kneel down to lay it out on the floor after moving aside the objects that are in the way. The pale blue paper is very thin and it has now taken on the dimensions of a plane occupying the entire width of the passageway. It must reveal where the treasure is hidden. The breeze coming in through the window lifts it up. I place a weight on each of its four corners. Having first to solve these difficulties merely piques my desire to read it, and I finally begin to do so, sprawled out with my elbows resting on the floor.

It is a long letter, in cramped handwriting, addressed to me. It bears no date. My body is hiding the place where the signature must be. I change position, consumed with curiosity, thereby revealing a blurred, indecipherable initial. The ink appears to have run, as though a tear had fallen on it. I look in bewilderment at the smudged capital letter and then stretch out on top of the large sheet again, sliding farther and farther down as I read. Someone is writing me that he's sitting on a beach, someone who says the immensity he has before him and the freedom to choose any itinerary he likes depress him because they remind him of my absence, which is apparently irreversible. It would appear from his allusions to the subject that this freedom that now seems empty to him has been something that he has fervently desired during a previous stage in which I am involved. It's a man writing because the adjectives that refer to him are in the masculine gender— "mutilated, reduced to nothing without you." He is gazing at the horizon and begins to call to me again and again. There are several lines consisting of nothing but my name, written between dashes and in small letters, with crests and troughs imitating the ocean waves. I allow myself to be lulled by the rippling lines that call me, as the sound of the real waves carried off with them the echo of his call from the shore. He says so a little further on, and from the literary point of view it is very expressive. He also reports that he is unable to calculate the time that he has spent reciting my name, nor does it matter, because from this moment onward time will never again count for anything with him. Then he gets up and begins to stroll idly down the deserted beach, allowing himself to get his feet wet. He notices that there are many fragments of broken dolls, arms, heads, trunks, legs, lying strewn about on the beach. Some of these remains come in on the tide. He describes the phenomenon as though it did not strike him as odd. He goes on walking, he disappears in the distance with his shoes in his hand. He does not appear to be carrying any other impedimenta.

I am sorry to see him wandering off in the distance before I manage to make out exactly what he looks like. Is he tall? How old is he? The beach is easier to imagine because all beaches look more or less alike. It might be the same one where I amused myself making drawings a while ago. If real time and that of dreams coincided, there would be a possibility that he would meet me a little farther on. Before reaching the last rocks he would stop, he would ask me why I was drawing a house, a bedroom, and a bed, and I would say to him: "If you want me to tell you, sit down, because it's a very long story," and I'd go on telling about them aloud, thus rescuing from oblivion all the things I've been remembering and heaven only knows how many more. There's no way of calculating how many ramifications a story will take on once one spies a gleam of attention in another's eyes. He too would surely be eager to tell me things. He would sit down at my side, we would begin to exchange memories the way children exchange little colored cards, and twilight would fall without our noticing. An intriguing, rambling story would come out, a tissue of truths and lies, like all stories. "All that calling to me"—I would say to him—"and you see, I was here all the time, less than a kilometer away. It's lucky you chanced to stroll to this end of the beach instead of heading for the other end." And we would talk about chance, in this sort of encounter one always speaks of chance, chance that forms the warp and woof of life and determines the plot of stories. The sun would set. Though it could also be that he wouldn't recognize me, because the times, of course, don't coincide. Perhaps he'd stroll by indifferently, lost in contemplation of his footprints, and I wouldn't be surprised either. Why would I be surprised? I would merely think: "Where can this man who's so pensive be going, carrying his shoes in his hand?"

I wonder who he can be and when and from where he can have written me. Years ago, I sometimes used to write myself apocryphal letters. I would keep them under lock and key for a while and then drop them in the mailbox with my own address on them. But this isn't my handwriting, though it does look vaguely familiar to me. . . . I can't rack my brains any more, my head is splitting. Where can the Optalidón pills have disappeared to? The floor has filled up with broken dolls whose remains have mingled with the objects that have spilled out of the sewing basket and gotten caught in turn in the tangle of multicolored threads. As the difficulty of the hieroglyph increases, my desire to understand it trickles away. The tide has suddenly surged over the beach in an unexpected swell and is sweeping everything away as it recedes. I admit defeat and give up. The barefoot man has now disappeared from sight.

Now the little girl from the provinces who can't manage to fall asleep is looking at me in the light of the little yellow lamp, whose bright glow has been dimmed by putting a handkerchief over it. She sees this bedroom drawn by Emilio Freixas on a glossy page in half-tones, the big unmade bed and the woman in pajamas reading a love letter on the rug. Her eyes gleam, she is imagining my distress. I am seeing her just as she is seeing me. In order that my image may recompose itself and not be swept away by the receding tide, I need to seek hospitality from that impatient, sleepless heart, that is to say my own heart. I perceive to my amazement that it is the same as always. I feel my chest, there it is, it is still beating in the same place, synchronized with my pulse at wrists and temples. I note the fact with voluptuous pleasure. I do not believe that the heart increases very much in size with age. It is subject to unknown disturbances. They say that tobacco smoke adversely affects it, just as excessive emotional stress does, but who can see this? These are subtle changes that stealthily creep up on us. Our growth was more immediately evident, betrayed by the fact that from one year to the next the hems of our dresses had to be let down or that our shoes from the previous winter began to pinch. But I don't believe the heart grows, it's simply that when it stops it stops. The important thing is for it not to stop. Sometimes doctors show you tracings that correspond to its strange adventures and in whose ups and downs they decipher an obscure destiny, just as though they were reading the lines of your palm— "You have a very good heart"—and we are amazed that those peaks and valleys have something to do with our anxieties, our disappointments, our enthusiasms. Tick-tock . . . it's still wound up. I've had rather good luck with that vital organ, with its auricles and ventricles that I drew on the blackboard of that schoolroom with dirty windows when my name was called to recite the Natural Sciences lesson. My name was also the same then, short and common. I had no idea that it could have that nice a sound on being uttered by a man on the beach. I would rather have been named Esperanza or Esmeralda or Elisabeth, like Elisabeth Mulder. Names with long exotic E's were popular. Mine didn't surpirse anybody, it began with the C of *cuarto, casa, cama* and of that *corazón* that I drew in chalk beneath the bored gaze of the teacher, the heart that raced when Norma Shearer kissed Leslie Howard, the one with an arrow through it that sweethearts carved into the trees of the Alamedilla, the one edged in red that men of the Foreign Legion wore underneath their battle jackets ("Stop, bullet, the heart of Jesus is with me"), the one that inevitably turned up in the boleros they played on the radio and in the titles of novels *(The Heart Doesn't Change, The Pitfalls of the Heart, Fearless Hearts)*. How much talk there has been of the heart! But how few times, on the other hand, do we stop to render it real homage, to think that it alone runs all the risks and keeps us alive. Here I am, my friend, still bearing up, like a good helmsman. How valiant, how humble, and how unknown, without ever once ceasing your endless toil, tick-tock, tick-tock.

The little girl lets the magazine fall to the floor and turns out the little yellow lamp. She is getting sleepy and I am too. I lie down on top of the letter. The stars move faster and faster and I have just enough time to say: "I want to see you, I want to see you," with my eyes closed. But I have no idea who it is I'm saying that to.

тНЕ blAck HAT

I AM AWAKENED by the telephone ringing. I fumble about with a start and pick it up, not knowing where I've picked it up from, and an unknown male voice utters my first and last names in a self-assured tone of voice in which a certain irritation is quite evident. I turn on the light: "Yes, this is she, but what's going on?" And as I hear him say that he's been knocking on the door for a long time and that now he's telephoning me from the bar downstairs, I realize that I'm lying in the big bed and that when I turned the light on I knocked over a glass of water on the night table and the top of the sheet has gotten soaking wet. Todorov's book, which is lying on the bedspread with some papers on top of it, has gotten all wet too. I hastily dry it off with my pajama sleeve.

"May I ask you what time it is?" I say to him.

He answers that it's 12:30 A.M., that that was the time I had set for the interview. I don't know what interview he's talking about, but I don't dare admit this. His tone of voice is imperious. He doesn't apologize for having awakened me, though he must be aware that he has. Apparently I had assured him that I'm always awake till very late at night. He says that if I prefer he'll go away and come back some other time.

"No, don't go. I'm wide awake," I assure him with incomprehensible conviction, as though my honor depended on maintaining this fiction. "It's just that it's very hard to hear the doorbell in this room in the back. It's one of those apartments with many long hallways, do you know the sort? But now I'll be expecting you. Come up whenever you like."

"The thing is, I don't see the night watchman, and what with all this rain. . . ."

I look toward the window, which is still half open, and note that a torrential, driving rain is indeed falling on the tiles of the terrace.

"Well then, wait a minute and I'll come downstairs to let you in."

I hurriedly take off my pajamas, put on a pair of pants, a T-shirt, sandals, grab up the keys, cross the sitting room. When I reach the doorway, half covered with a red curtain, that leads to the hall, I stop for a few seconds before turning on the light, with the presentiment that a cockroach is going to appear. I fearfully turn on the light switch, and no more than a yard away from my feet there's an enormous, totally motionless cockroach, standing out clearly in the center of one of the white tiles, as though certain that it is occupying the square it belongs in on a gigantic chessboard. The worst of it is that it doesn't move, though it's obvious that my presence is no more of a surprise to it than its presence is to me.

This is a source of strength to it. Its plan seems to be to keep me from getting past it. I don't know how long we remain there confronting each other, both of us paralyzed, as though trying to decipher each other's intentions. Finally I reject all intention of attacking it and opt for that of fleeing from it: I start running, leaping over its body, which is very nearly the size of a rat's, and it follows me in a sinuous stagger. As I round the second turn in the hall, I stop looking behind me, reach the entryway thoroughly shaken, slam the door shut behind me, step out onto the landing, consider myself safe and sound. Leaning against the wall in the dark, alongside the elevator shaft, I try my best to calm down and wait for my breathing to return to normal. It was enormous. It seemed to be staring at me. Will it be lying in wait for me? Luckily, when I come back in, I won't be alone, a man's company is always good protection.

The light in the stairwell has gone on all of a sudden. I walk over toward the elevator to summon it, but don't reach it in time because the red arrow has lit up all by itself. I stand there with my finger in the air next to the row of buttons. The elevator is coming upstairs. Will it come up here? It must be him. I wait with mingled fear and anxiety, as before seeing the cockroach appear. The arrow doesn't blink out. The elevator is still on its way up, it's coming, it must already have passed the sixth floor . . . and the seventh. The sound of it is close now. Here it is. It stops and a man dressed in black steps out of it and stands there looking straight at me. He is tall and is wearing a broad-brimmed hat, also black.

"The night watchman finally turned up," he says.

And he holds out a big, thin, rather cold hand to me. After shaking it, my own hand trembles slightly as I insert the key in the lock. I turn on the light in the entryway.

"Please come in," I say to him.

I walk down the hallway in front of him, without turning around, in silence. Before rounding the first corner, I halt abruptly and his body collides with my back. I am overpowered. I look at him, unable to take a step farther. I didn't think he was following that close behind me.

"Excuse me, it's just that there was an enormous cockroach here before and it gave me a scare," I say. "It doesn't seem to be here now. It must have gone into the kitchen."

At the end of this stretch of hallway is the sitting room, enveloped in a reddish glow. I walked on, looking apprehensively at the black and white tiles.

"Cockroaches are harmless," I hear his voice say behind me. "Moreover, their bodies have a shininess, a gleam to them that's very attractive. People have too many prejudices against them."

We have reached the sitting room. I part the curtain and allow him to precede me into the room, with neither of us saying a word. The door that opens onto my bedroom, closed off with a half-drawn matching curtain, has been left ajar. The man — noting this with a certain uneasiness — walks over to it and stands there contemplating a picture hanging on the wall next to the entrance to the bedroom. It is entitled "The World Turned Topsy-Turvy" and consists of forty-eight rectangles, printed in black on a yellow background, in which absurd scenes are depicted, as for example a man with a scythe in his hand making threatening gestures at Death, which is fleeing in terror, fish flying through the air above a sea where horses and lions are swimming, a sheep with a hat and a shepherd's crook herding two peasants, a little boy on all fours with a chair on top of him, and the sun and the moon stuck fast in the earth beneath a sky full of buildings. It was a crude print on cheap paper that somebody bought once for two pesetas in a village in Andalusia. He gave it to me as a gift and I had it encased in plastic and set in a gilt frame. The man contemplates it attentively, then turns around, removes his hat, which is quite wet, and asks me with a questioning look whether he may leave it on the table, and I nod. His hair is very black, and rather long. His eyes are very black too and gleam like two cockroaches.

"So you're afraid of cockroaches," he says.

"Yes, especially when I think they're about to appear. What terrifies me most is the way they have of turning up just as one is thinking of them, and starting to race about as fast as their legs can carry them. They're unpredictable."

"They're mysterious," he concedes. "Like all apparitions. Don't you like mystery stories?"

He has left his hat, like a temporary paperweight, on top of a pile of papers lying next to the typewriter. All his gestures seem like a slow-motion film sequence.

"Mystery stories? Yes I do. That's a literary genre I've always liked very much. Why do you ask?"

"Because it's not one you practice."

He has sat down without my inviting him to do so, in the left-hand corner of the sofa. I have remained standing, next to the table on which he has just deposited his hat. A page already begun is peeking out of the top of the typewriter, and I read out of the corner of my eye: ". . . The barefoot man has now disappeared from sight." When did I write that? I had the impression that I'd left the typewriter with the cover over it. I've been having lapses of memory a lot lately. As though to make contact with reality, I look closely at my visitor, who has stretched out his legs and is exploring the room from where he is seated with a mixture of interest, calm deliberation, and aloofness. I try to concentrate on the last thing he has said, and have the feeling that too much time has gone by since he said it.

"Well, my first novel was rather mysterious," I say, with a certain bewilderment, my gaze once again fixed on the table that I am leaning on. The sheets of paper that the hat has left visible also have writing on them, some of it in longhand and some of it typed. They form a pile of fifteen pages or so. It's been so long since I've written anything that I am extremely curious. What I would like most would be to sit down and have a look at them, but the man's voice banishes all thought of my doing so.

"I beg your pardon, I didn't hear what you said very well. You speak in a very low voice."

"Yes, I have trouble pitching my voice properly," I say, raising it. "Sometimes I speak too loudly and at other times too softly."

"That happens to everyone who's hard of hearing," he remarks in the same offhanded way in which he stated that cockroaches are mysterious. "Are you hard of hearing?"

"Yes, I have been for some time now."

All of a sudden the atmosphere is charged with that peculiar tenseness that makes itself felt in doctors' offices before they begin to ask questions about the symptoms of our illness. I am surprised to find myself telling him exactly that.

"I have the most trouble hearing when I'm lying down."

And then I stop short, realizing how absurd that sentence is, and also because I have the impression that he is looking at me with a more or less mocking expression in his eyes.

"That's why I didn't hear you when you rang at the door before," I hurriedly add. "Because I was lying down."

I stand there lost in thought again. When the telephone woke me up I was stretched out on the bed. Yes, that's right, I tipped the glass of water over. But before that? Before that I'd fallen asleep on the floor, on top of a blue letter. I look over toward the curtain over the bedroom doorway, my mind a blank, as always when I've lost something and in order to find it try my best to retrace my blurred footprints in the fog ("Did I go out?" "Did I go to the kitchen?" "I think I had my keys in my hand"). It's a situation in whose toils I find myself imprisoned very often. How much time wasted, how many useless wanderings back and forth through this apartment, down through the years, searching for something. What am I searching for now? Ah, yes, the track of time. As always, time is what gets lost most often, a stretch beyond recovery between the disappearance of the man on the beach and the telephone call from this other man. "The barefoot man has now disappeared from sight." Of course! That's the answer, I must have come out here and begun to write to see if I could drive my insomnia away.

"Why don't you come over here and sit down?" the man in black asks me, pointing to a place at his side on the sofa, as though he were the master of the house and I the visitor.

I obey mechanically, still absorbed in my conjectures, which fall apart as though they'd come unbasted as I move away from the table. Perhaps the whole secret lies in losing the thread and it will reappear again when it jolly well pleases. I've always been too afraid of losing the thread. I cross the room and sit down beside him. The journey has seemed to me to be a long one, as though I had had to skirt many obstacles that stood in my way.

"In which ear is your hearing best?" he asks me. "One's hearing is always better in one ear than in the other, isn't that true?"

"Yes. In the right one."

I see that he rises politely to his feet and sits down again on my right. I automatically sit up straighter and slide over to the corner of the sofa. We'd ended up sitting too close together.

"What were you saying?" he goes on. "That you were writing a mystery novel?"

"Right now? . . . No, not at present, I haven't written anything for some time," I say, glancing, uneasy still, in the direction of the table where I can still see the pile of papers with writing on them lying next to his hat.

The forearm of this unknown visitor rises before my eyes, in a slow and rather solemn gesture. It stops in midair and a thin wrist appears below the sleeve of his jacket. His index finger straightens and points to the table.

"What do you mean you haven't been writing? What about that over there?"

There is a brief silence and my heart begins to pound. The rain beats against the panes of the French door opposite us that overlooks an open terrace.

"That? . . . It's nothing . . . I don't know."

"What do you mean you don't know? Isn't this your study?"

"Well, yes, I work in here sometimes, though I don't have a special room set aside to work in."

"But that's your typewriter, isn't it?"

"Yes."

"Well then, try to remember. It's obvious that you're writing something."

All this sounds like a police interrogation. I can't bear being cross-examined till I'm backed into a corner.

"Please drop the subject. I tell you I don't know."

I have said this in an impatient tone of voice. His arm descends, disappearing from my visual field, and I feel slightly relieved. But my feeling of relief is a temporary one. In a quiet, impassive voice, he returns to the attack.

"Well, let's see. You don't know what it is you're writing, you say? That's very odd."

His insistence makes me feel unduly irritated. Moreover, his last sentence has coincided with a blinding flash of lightning above the terrace railing. This is sheer happenstance, I know very well, but it nonetheless contributes to making me all the more furious. Escaping my control, my voice suddenly explodes, in unison with the burst of thunder that follows.

"That's enough. Leave me alone! I don't know, I really don't. I've already told you that I don't know, that I don't remember anything!"

The echo of the two discharges lingers in the air. I am immediately ashamed of myself. I look at him, intending to apologize, and see, to my surprise, that he is smiling.

"Well, that's certain proof at least," he says.

"Certain proof . . . of what?"

"That you don't remember anything."

"I don't understand what you mean."

"Never mind. Certain things are beyond understanding.

Every time I lose my temper the same thing happens. My irritation at once silently turns against me. I feel it churning round and round in my stomach, unable to settle down, like something I've eaten that I'm having difficulty digesting. The only thing that would calm me down would be to stretch out for a while on the sofa and close my eyes, but this strange presence keeps me from doing so. The substitute for rest is compulsive activity, although this never works: pretending that one is attending to some urgent task and allowing oneself to get all caught up in it. I rise to my feet, walk over to the venetian blind, perhaps to lower it, to shut out the sight of more flashes of lightning.

"What's the matter? Are you afraid of the storm?"

His voice, at my back, has sounded solicitous, kindly now. It hasn't seemed strange to me. I turn away from the French door and my heart stops pounding.

"Sometimes, when I'm nervous . . ."

"I see. Are you nervous now?"

It seems as though the question really interests him. He gives no sign of wanting to pry. His intention would appear, rather, to be to shed light on the subject, to be of help. I shrug.

"Did the cockroach make you nervous?" he asks insistently.

I drop my defensive attitude, smile at him.

"Certain things are beyond understanding," I say simply.

"I agree. But come here, don't lower the blind. When there's a storm, it's better to watch it."

His words interrupted me just as I had grabbed the cord and was about to lower the blind. I walk back toward him confidently, feeling that we've made our peace with each other. In front of the sofa is a low table with a pack of cigarettes on it. I take a cigarette out of it. My fingers tremble slightly. The stranger stretches out his arm and offers me a light with an old-fashioned lighter, the kind with a big yellow wick. The flame blazes up, I lean over, and our heads are now close together. I note an odd odor about him, as though he used a lotion with a tar base.

"Wait, you're going to singe your hair," he says, brushing aside a lock of it that was falling over my face. "Did you get a light?"

"Yes, thanks."

I sit down again and we watch the rain, neither of us saying a word.

"I love storms," he finally says.

"I used to like them a lot too when I was little. I was just a bit afraid of them, but it was a different sort of fear."

I lean my head against the back of the sofa. The prayer that we used to recite each time a flash of lightning appeared on the horizon has just come back to me:

Santa Bárbara bendita
que en el cielo estás escrita
*con papel y agua bendita.**

All my cousins and I were in the summerhouse in Galicia. We had a kerosene lamp for light. The storm grappled with the mountain peaks. I liked to go out onto the back stairs alone to get wet, to feel the rain lashing the hazelnut trees in the garden, to smell the damp earth. They called me, they searched for me, they scolded me. I was more afraid to go in than I was to stay outside. I was afraid of being shut in, afraid of the others, and what I was afraid of most of all was praying.

"Don't be so sure it was a different sort of fear," the man says. "Nobody has ever had any idea what fear is. We talk about it just to hear ourselves talk."

"Yes, we talk about almost all our emotions just to hear ourselves talk, out of fear of confronting the naked truth of them."

"Of course," he says. "Out of fear of fear."

And the terrace is illuminated by another flash of lightning. I puff on the cigarette. Preciosa, Cervantes's Little Gypsy Girl, had a spell for warding off heart troubles and dizzy spells:

*Blessed Saint Barbara / your name is written in heaven / with paper and holy water. (*Translator's note.*)

Cabecita, cabecita,
tente a ti, no te resbales
y apareja los puntales
de la paciencia bendita.

Verás cosas
que toquen en milagrosas
Dios delante
y San Cristóbal gigante. *

It has always calmed me like a magic incantation. The most important thing that one can ask for is for one's head not to slip away, especially if one asks it of one's own head.

"That burst of thunder was even louder," the man says. "The storm is upon us."

I close my eyes, overcome by a sudden languor. This way, with my eyes closed, I can imagine that he is a friend I've known all my life, someone I've met again after a long absence.

"Are you all right? Or are you still afraid?"

"No, no."

I smile with my eyes closed.

"Oh, Raimundo," Esperanza exclaimed, as the tears flowed from beneath her closed eyelids. "I'm never afraid when I'm with you. Never go away." That was from a novel published as a serial in *Lecturas*. That sentence was written, as the style

---

*Little head, little head, / keep hold of yourself, don't slip away / and ready the props / of blessed patience. / You will see things / that are well-nigh miraculous / God before you / and giant Saint Christopher. *(Translator's note.)*

was then, at the bottom of one of the illustrations, which showed a woman with her head leaning against the back of a sofa and a man bending solicitously over her. In another earlier illustration the two of them had not yet sat down on that sofa, the room was the same one but they were sitting facing each other, in a more tense and circumspect attitude, the woman with her legs crossed and a glass in her hand. It said underneath: "Esperanza and Raimundo looked at each other in sad amazement." It's as though I can see that drawing this minute, foreshadowing the tears of the reunion. How fond I was of romantic novels.

"Well, we could go on discussing fantastic literature—what better occasion than a stormy night? Let's do that, if you feel like it. . . ."

I nod without opening my eyes. Let him begin wherever he wants to. I'd like not to talk any more. I wish I dared lean my head on his shoulder. I concentrate on this idea, which excites me, but immediately it is besieged by an army of reasons charged with safeguarding normality and warding off the danger. They rush to the fore to surround the temptation like a swarm of antibodies. A brief and intense struggle begins that is an old story to me. In the end, my head doesn't move, as was only to be expected: yielding to temptation has always been more difficult for me than overcoming it.

He says nothing, seemingly in no hurry to attack the subject that he has suggested. I am aware of his fingers approaching mine and removing my cigarette, which no doubt has burned down close to the end. He must be stubbing it out in the ashtray. My pleasant languor has turned into a feeling of tension, into something uncomfortable. Sitting there quietly, in silence, with my eyes closed, is beginning to be like insisting on winning a bet I've made with myself. The one who's most indifferent always holds out the longest.

"Please tell me what you're thinking about," I finally say, as though admitting defeat.

"Nothing in particular," I hear him say in an imperturbable voice. "I was looking at this room. It's charming."

I open my eyes and feel that I've come floating up to the surface again, safe and sound. It's as though someone had blindfolded me to surprise me and then said to me: "Now you can look." The room in fact does strike me as a very pretty one, as though I were seeing it for the first time in my life. What I like most is the red wallpaper, that covers the ceiling as well. Sometimes I have dreams in which my life has just been in great danger—storms, shipwrecks, getting hopelessly lost—and someone takes me by the hand and leads me to a safe place, brings me to a brightly glowing fire. My feeling at this moment is somewhere between that one in the dreams and the one in the blindfold game: a feeling of return and of relief. I would like to tell him that I'm not afraid any more—"Oh, Raimundo, I'm never afraid when I'm with you"—that I'm grateful to him for having brought me to this room. There is always a dreamed text, vague and fleeting, that precedes the one that is actually recited and is swept away by it.

"It would be nice if there were a fireplace," I say, looking toward the table where he has put his hat down. "Over there, in that corner, don't you think so?"

"Yes. Why don't you have one installed there?"

"I never thought of it before. The idea just now occurred to me all of a sudden."

"Well, it wouldn't be hard to do, since this is the top floor of the building, isn't it?"

"Yes."

"It would draw well."

I shrug.

"Perhaps so, but it really doesn't matter. I'm just not up to having major renovations made and the house turned topsy-turvy."

The fireplace dreamed of—that for a few moments had materialized in the corner with its crackling logs, swallowing up the pages that I don't remember having written and encouraging a conversation about fantastic literature with the stranger who has brought me to the refuge—vanishes and the room turns back into the same one that it has always been, with all its weight of memories and echoes of the past. The man now gazes once again in the direction of the typewriter.

"Do you always work here?"

"No, I very often move from one place to another. Sometimes, expecially if I've gotten bogged down, taking my papers to another room perks me up. It has the same effect on me as traveling to another city, and since I travel very little . . ."

"Why is that? Don't you like to travel?"

"Yes I do, but it's something I never deliberately plan in advance on doing. I need to feel a sudden urge to go somewhere. I think that journeys should just happen to come your way, like friends, like books, like all the rest. What I fail to understand is the obligation to travel, or to read, or to meet people. All I need is for somebody to say to me: 'You'll be absolutely delighted to make the acquaintance of so-and-so,' or 'You really must read Joyce,' or 'You have to see the Grand Canyon before you die' for me to feel immediately put off, precisely because what I really like is discovering things for myself. People nowadays travel because it's the thing to do, and when they come back they don't have anything to say. The farther they go, the fewer things they turn out to have seen. Traveling has lost its mystery."

"That's not true," he says. "We're the ones who have shorn it of its mystery. Man today profanes mysteries by rushing about all over the globe with travel guides and fixed itineraries, by vaingloriously shrinking the distance between one place and another, without realizing that only distance can reveal the secret of what seemed to be hidden."

As he has uttered this last sentence, he has been looking at me with a different, enigmatic expression, as if he were hinting at something else. And this disturbs me because it reminds me of something that someone else once said to me.

"Yes . . . distance," I say, as though endeavoring, in vain, to bring back to mind this hesitant memory.

"What about distance?"

I look at him. His face is once again that of a stranger. Immediately, following his example, I deliberately allow an expression of complete indifference to come over my own face once again. I give up the search, I return to the text.

"Nothing, simply that you're right, that everything nowadays is too close at hand. Once upon a time the difficulties involved in getting places was the greatest incentive for traveling; so many preparations; trips began long before one started out on them. Good Lord, what going to another country meant! How passionately we desired such a thing. It's as though I can still see my first passport. When I finally got it, I slept with it under my pillow every night before the journey. I think that that's why I got so much pleasure out of everything back then."

"It might also be because you were younger."

"Yes, of course, I was just twenty years old. But do you think that people who are twenty years old today leave the country with the same keen anticipation?"

"Possibly not. Where did you go?"

"To Coimbra. I'd been awarded a scholarship. But many things had to be arranged beforehand—my irregular situation, first of all, with regard to my Social Service. A girl couldn't leave the country without having completed her Social Service, or at the very least having given a good indication, during the course of her studies at the university, that she had the makings of a good future wife and mother, a worthy descendant of Queen Isabella."

"And you didn't have the makings?"

"Obviously not. At least the reports on me weren't very satisfactory. I had to sign a paper promising to pay a sort of fine, which consisted of completing several more months of service on my return."

"And you signed it?"

"Yes, of course. That's why I spoke of the keen anticipation of leaving the country. If you only knew how horrible the prospect of completing my Social Service seemed to me, you'd understand better why I willingly went through all the necessary red tape. Convincing my father was another obstacle. It was the first time in my life that I'd be traveling by myself. But anyway, I managed to persuade him too. I pulled out all the stops, let me tell you, I wasn't going to let anything stand in my way. I should also add that, perhaps as a compensation for all that enthusiasm, the trip didn't disappoint me. Portugal seemed to me to be the most exotic and the most distant country on earth."

"Portugal has always been a long way away," the man in black says, "possibly because of the very fact of its physical closeness, though this is doubtless a mirage."

Far away, yes, very far away. It is summer, we are on an excursion in a yellow bus. Someone has been telling the story of Doña Inés de Castro, kept prisoner in the Quinta del Mondego. The bus stops. We have arrived at Amarante, we get out there, there are many vineyards. How could a place called Amarante not be far away, since it sounds like a name straight out of a novel of chivalry or a fairy story? I am wearing a white piqué suit with a square neckline and padded shoulders. As soon as we get off the bus they give us wine. I begin to sing a *fado,* very softly:

Faz o ninho n'a outra banda
*deix en paz meu coração**

"How quickly you've learned that *fado!*" says the scholarship student from Madrid, a pale-eyed girl who shared my room in

*Make your nest on the other shore / leave my heart in peace. *(Translator's note.)*

the residence where we had met, run by little nuns near the Penedo da Saudade. Two Portuguese boys we didn't know came to sing this *fado* under our window every night. They also sent us poems and letters signed with just one initial. They intrigued us and contrived to keep us in suspense. It took us a long time to get to meet them. Affairs of the heart were a very slow process in Portugal, conducted according to an age-old ritual whereby absence makes the heart grow fonder.

"Surely there was someone you loved in Portugal," the man in black says.

"Yes. A boy from Oporto, an engineering student, who came to sing *fados* beneath my window. When we saw each other for the first time he was going away the next day and bade me farewell. We said goodbye to each other many times more. Every time we saw each other was a farewell, but he never did go away. And that was what kept me spellbound. The fact that I thought he was about to go away."

"A very Portuguese story, that."

"It certainly is. After that, he kept writing me letters to Salamanca for years. For a long time I kept them in a little tin chest that had once belonged to my mother. That young man wrote very well, but he never came to see me. It all remained on a very poetic plane. He used to say that anyone who endeavored to speak of spring without having known me would have a false idea of it. I'm sorry now that I burned those letters of his."

"And why was it you burned them?"

"I don't know. I've burned so many things — letters, diaries, poetry. I get sudden attacks of pyromania sometimes; old scraps of paper depress me. Because after you've fingered them for such a long time, they become emptied of all their content; they cease to be what they once were."

I fall silent. I held my last great pyromaniac session one afternoon in February. I had been reading Machado in this very room and suddenly I fell into a rage. But I'd already burned the letters from the Portuguese boy before that, perhaps when I moved away from Salamanca, or else they got lost somehow, I don't remember.

"The most terrifying thing about old letters is when one has forgotten where one has put them for safekeeping or when one doesn't even know if one has kept them, and then suddenly they reappear," the man says thoughtfully. "It's as though someone from another planet were giving us back a slice of our life."

I look at him in confusion, thinking of the man on the beach. His letter must have been written after my auto-da-fé in February. Or perhaps I spared it from the fire because it seemed too beautiful to burn, who knows.

"I don't find that terrifying," I say. "Reappearances of that sort seem miraculous to me."

"Everything miraculous is a little terrifying. Incidentally, we've gone on with our conversation without pursuing the subject of the fantastic as a literary genre."

"Don't be so certain. Fantastic literature has a great deal to do with letters that reappear."

"With those that disappear, you mean?"

"With those that disappear as well."

"And what happened to the little tin chest?"

"I gave it away several years ago."

"With nothing in it, I presume."

"That's right, with nothing in it. After the last fire, I didn't use it any more. It was all the fault of Don Antonio Machado."

"Don Antonio Machado? I can't believe it!"

"It's true though. I was reading poems of his in this very room . . . well anyway, the room was the same, but not the furniture. This sofa didn't exist, for example, and there was a table here that I now have in the kitchen. The book was lying on it, and all of a sudden I came to a poem that says:

No guardes en tu cofre la galana
veste dominical, el limpio traje
para llenar de lágrimas mañana
la mustia seda y el marchito encaje . . .*

I don't know if you recall it."

I look at him, and there is an intense gleam in his eyes.

"Why wouldn't I remember? "

To recall and to remember are words with a different shade of meaning; by saying that he remembers, he seems to be referring to the scene on that February afternoon rather than to Machado's text. I lower my eyes.

"And what happened?"

"Well, nothing, just that I saw myself hurtled into old age, doomed to the vice of endlessly reading over letters that had lost all their fragrance, with the ink blurred from their being

---

*Do not keep in your chest the elegant / Sunday attire, the clean dress, / only to drench with tears tomorrow / the musty silk and the faded lace . . . (Translator's note.)

40

handled so much and having been wept over so often, and I was overcome with a frantic rage to destroy papers, the like of which I can't recall ever having experienced before. I rose to my feet and began taking out letters and dumping out everything in the little chest. I piled it all up out there in the hallway and without looking at any of it threw every last bit into the stove that heated the apartment. It took me all of an hour and the flames blazed higher with each handful. Heaven only knows how many treasures disappeared in that holocaust."

I have been sitting there looking at that same hallway, through the doorway with the red curtain over it. That crematorium isn't even there any more. The place where the stove was looks whiter now.

"We heated with coal back then," I explain.

The man's eyes have followed mine. I try to imagine how this apartment must look to him. I wonder if I, who think I know it so well, have ever seen it as it looks to him now. One never gets to the bottom of the secret of what is close at hand.

"Have you lived here for a long time?"

"Since '53."

I heave a sigh. I have caught hold of the thread again, as always happens when I remember a date. Dates are the milestones of routine.

"That was the very same year," I go on, "that I began to write my first novel, the one that is rather mysterious, as I was telling you before . . . when you didn't hear me."

It was this same apartment, yes, I remember the gray light that came through the window of a little bedroom in it, to the right on the way out. It had practically no furniture, the sewing machine was in there. I opened a notebook with oil-cloth covers and wrote: "We arrived this afternoon, after a bus ride of several hours. . . ." I didn't have a very good idea of how I was going to go on from there, but I liked this beginning. I sat there looking out of the window with my pen in the air. It was about to rain.

"What novel was that?" he says. "The one that's set in a spa?"

I seem to note a certain disappointment in his voice.

"Yes, that one. Don't you think it has a certain air of mystery about it?"

"Yes, it could have been a good fantastic novel," he says slowly. "It had a very promising beginning, but then you allowed fear to overcome you, a fear you've never lost. What happened to you?"

"I don't remember. Fear? . . . I don't know what you're talking about."

"Do you remember the arrival? . . . The arrival at the spa, I mean."

I nod my head slightly to show that I remember, a memory that has nothing whatsoever to do with the text of the year 1953 that seems to interest him, but goes back, rather, to its sources. Arriving at a spa always made me feel both anxious and excited. And I didn't understand why, since everything at a spa was so normal, a world steeped in tradition, surrounded by every sort of security, frequented by affable, well-bred people who smiled and politely greeted each other and were immediately disposed to welcome us within their circle, to exchange calling cards with us, an exchange that would give rise to enduring and obligatory friendships all during one's stay, sustained by such trivialities as a banal meeting in the hallways, on the stairs that led down to the spring, or in the game room. None of that seemed real to me. I felt that they were tricking me by making me recite with them the text of a theatrical play that to all appearances was harmless yet concealed secret dangers. And I tried my best to decipher some clear sign beneath those ritual gestures, those reassuring countenances. I was a young unmarried girl from the provinces. I had come there with my father, who suffered from kidney trouble. In two days' time everybody had begun to talk to us. They knew our names and addressed us freely by them in their conversations with us. They told us all about their illnesses, in great detail, during the quiet afternoons.

I remember one arrival in particular. We had come from Orense to the spa at Cabreiroá, in Verín, in a taxi. It was hot, and on the heights above one could see the castle of Monterrey, enveloped in reddish clouds. It was the summer of '44. I had just passed my first-year exams in Philosophy and Letters. We entered a leafy park, stopped in front of the façade of the spa, and as a bellboy removed our baggage from the taxi, I stood there motionless looking at him, with a feeling of intense strangeness. I had a big square white leather bag with a long strap slung over my shoulder. My father had given it to me a month before as a present for passing my exams. I took out the little pocket mirror inside it, looked at myself, and spied in the rectangle the eyes of someone I didn't recognize, staring at me intently. I saw that the bellboy, a youngster my age, was looking at me with a smile on his face that embarrassed me a little. I pretended to be removing a speck of dirt from my eye, but the disturbing thought crossed my mind that I wasn't me. Just as that place wasn't that place. And I had a sort of premonition: "This is literature. I am being possessed by literature."

"What is most successful is the feeling of strangeness. You arrive with your companion, you stand together next to the railing of that bridge looking at the green water with the mill in the distance. The germ of the fantastic is already contained in that passage, and during the entire first part you manage to maintain that atmosphere. One doesn't know whether that man who is with you exists or not, whether he knows you well or not. That is what is really essential, daring to face up to uncertainty. And the reader feels that he can neither believe nor fail to believe what is going to happen from then on. That is the basis of fantastic literature. It's a question of rejecting everything there in that hotel that subsequently seems perversely bent on appearing to you to be altogether normal and obvious, isn't that so?"

"Yes . . . I think it was something like that."

That night in the dining room, I spied a family that looked quite refined: a father with four children, two girls and two boys. I don't remember the mother, though she may have been there with them too. At spas one hardly ever meets anybody but oldsters, so this family fascinated me, especially the elder son, who was wearing a white sweater and affecting an indifferent air. His brother and his sisters kept casting furtive glances in the direction of our table every so often, because at spas the arrival of new people is always an event. But this older brother didn't look at us even once. I saw him smoking, not saying a word, between courses, as I listened distractedly to what my father was saying: "Look, what luck. There are young people. You'll be able to make friends."

In the days that followed I made their acquaintance. They were from Madrid, people with money, and the father had a business interest in that spa. He was the manager, I think. I got to be rather good friends with the girls and the younger boy, but I saw less of the older one. He was in the habit of seeking out the company of adults, and on several afternoons he took part in a game of billiards in which my father also participated. He enjoyed displaying his ennui and that indifference that made him seem so attractive to me. He very seldom deigned to come down from his Olympus. He would come through the salon as though he were looking for something or someone as we younger ones were playing a game of matrimony or forfeits. Perhaps he'd come over with a message for his brother and sisters, and then after he'd disappeared, everything became unbearably dull again. One night, however, he came over and leaned on the piano in the salon where the house piano player, a good-looking widow, was playing boleros and other popular songs of the day, and remained in that position for some time. He had on a sleeveless V-neck sweater in brown tones and a white short-sleeved shirt. I was in one corner, joining in on the chorus of those songs along with the others, trying to sing them in as beautiful a voice as possible and fill them with hidden meaning. What I wanted was to keep him there and to get this across to him without my having to tell him so. I remember the moment that I dared raise my face and cast a bold glance in his direction, catching his eyes staring directly into mine. Nor can I forget the words of the song within which, as in some forbidden, secret place, our eyes spoke to each other:

Ven, que te espero en el Cairo,
junto a la orilla del Nilo;
la noche africana,
sensual y pagana,
será testigo mudo de nuestro amor . . . *

As I remember, it was a song from a review that had had a fair success at the time and the title of it was "Honeymoon in Cairo." That was ecstasy, the culmination of all the novels that had fed my adolescent imagination. The place was no longer the same, it had been transformed into the salon of a passenger liner. We were sailing into the infinite and the lights wheeled round and round. The dullness of the postwar period had disappeared, that continual need to watch every penny and think of an uncertain future. Time didn't exist, nor was I there with my cautious, upright, reasonable father. The unexpected was possible. That was the first time I had ever dared look a man boldly in the eye, just because, because I liked him, and all the dreams, adventures, and torments of impossible love were concentrated in those few seconds. He must have realized what all

*Come, I'm waiting for you in Cairo, / on the shore of the Nile; / the African night, / sensual and pagan, / will be the silent witness of our love. . . . *(Translator's note.)*

46

that meant to me. He didn't so much as blink. Everything about him gave off a dark light of complicity, of shared desire. He was dragging me down to hell and I knew that he knew. I finally lowered my eyes in a state of utter intoxication, of sensual pleasure, and when I raised them again, after I don't know how long, another song was being played and he had left. From then on I saw him even less. I strolled about alone in the park at dusk dreaming of meeting him, I leaned against the trunk of a tree, I closed my eyes, I waited. "He has to come," I said to myself fearfully. "There's no way around it. He knows I'm waiting for him." But he never came nor did he ever look at me again as he had that night. The few times he spoke to me he seemed to make a special point of emphasizing the banality of the exchange, without so much as a trace of that furtive, intense, magnetic look. It was as though I'd dreamed it. Yet on the other hand I was certain I hadn't dreamed it, that I'd glimpsed it in his eyes. That was the worst part: the ambiguity. I lost myself in pointless conjectures.

"Ambiguity is the key to fantastic literature," the man in black says. "Not knowing whether what one has seen is true or false, never finding out. You should have dared to walk along that tightrope till the end of the story."

"Yes," I reluctantly concede. "You may be right."

I spent the evening before our departure writing him a rather wild farewell letter. I wasn't sure I'd dare give it to him, but writing it calmed me. The following morning I put on a pink and white dress that I liked a lot and wandered aimlessly about the hallways and galleries with that bit of paper in my pocket, postponing our meeting. I met various people who said hello and stopped to speak to me. I answered them politely, with a sort of Olympian condescension, knowing that I was in possession of a secret that they could never share, that I was capable of doing something unthinkable, since no decent and decorous young lady of that day would have had the audacity to write a letter like that. I went out into the park and read it all over. It was altogether literary. The person to whom it was addressed mattered not at all. I was in a transport of narcissism. I strode resolutely back into the hotel, and the moment I set foot in the lobby, I saw him from the back, talking with my father and several other gentlemen. I walked over. The presence of the others afforded me protection. I placed myself between my father and him. He smelled of "Dandy" aftershave lotion and was wearing a raw silk jacket. The whole trick was to take the letter out of my pocket and slip it into his. I might be able to do so almost without his noticing, if I was capable of doing such a thing. That look of love had really existed, and if it hadn't, it was like a wager, and at the same time it was something like a riddle. My fingers were trembling. At that moment I heard him mention Hitler's name. He was addressing me, showing me a newspaper: "Don't you know what's happened?" I grabbed it. Hitler had just been the victim of an attempt on his life from which he had miraculously escaped unharmed. The military officers who had organized the plot had all been shot to death. I stood there for a while without opening my mouth, without anyone paying any more attention to me. Reading that news that was so distant and unreal that all the older men, and he too, were commenting on it with aplomb, as though they regarded it as an event not worthy of serious discussion. "He's the greatest tyrant in history," my father said. I didn't care at all about the Germans. I didn't really understand why they'd come to Spain during our war, why they had been billeted in our houses. I didn't understand anything about wars and didn't have any desire to understand. I think now that Hitler's death in that month of July might have changed the course of history, but at the time I scorned history, and furthermore I didn't believe it, I didn't believe a word of what was recounted in history books or in the newspapers. Those who believed such things were to blame for what happened. I was sick and tired of hearing the words *shot to death*, the word *victim*, the word *tyrant*, the word *soldiers*, the word *fatherland*, the word *history*. I went up to my room, tore the letter up in a fit of rage, and that look was reduced to bits. It ended up swelling the flow down the drains of deception. I sat there on the bed for a long time without a single thought crossing my mind, looking in bewilderment at the open suitcase with my dresses spilling out of it. Then the bellboy knocked on the door and told me that my father was waiting for me. I recognized him, and he smiled. He was the one who had seen me peeking at myself in the little mirror on the afternoon we arrived. I have just realized that something of all this is what, years later, I tried to bring back to life in *The Spa*, when young Matilde awakens from her dream.

"Why insist on making it clear that it was a dream?" the man in black says. "You're too logical."

I look at him as though I had just awakened. He is in profile. I can't tell how old he is. He might well be the young man leaning on the piano. We confuse certain people with others in dreams.

"The second part, the one that begins with the awakening and continues with the realistic description of the spa, spoils everything. It is the fruit of fear. You strayed from the path of dreams."

He has said this in a reproachful tone of voice. Possibly he considers my later historical research as an even more serious betrayal of ambiguity. When I began it, I was aware that I was going astray, deserting dreams in order to come to a compromise with history, forcing myself to put things in order, to understand them one by one, out of fear of being shipwrecked.

"Literature is a defiance of logic," he goes on, "not a refuge against uncertainty."

Yes . . . uncertainty; he always hits the nail square on the head. On that very afternoon in the year 1953 when I began to write *The Spa,* uncertainty began to prey upon me. Like the bluebird of storms, it flew to my window from the attempt on Hitler's life, from that first look torn to bits.

"Do you think I take literature as a refuge?"

I have asked him that with some anxiety. It seems to me that I am holding out my open palm for him to read. His answer is as terse and solemn as a gypsy curse.

"Yes, of course, but it's of no avail to you."

"No refuge is of any avail, but one can't live out in the open."

"One can try."

"That would mean entering a labyrinth."

"A labyrinth, if you like, but not a fortified castle. One must choose between losing oneself and defending oneself."

I was about to answer him back, but I realize that that would be to continue to defend myself. Moreover, it would be a hopeless move, because he's a far more expert fencer than I am. I look at his black hat lying on the table like a sort of bird of ill omen, ready to crow over my defeat.

"Don't you ever defend yourself?" I ask him.

"Not any more," he says. "I gave up fortified castles long ago."

There is a silence, too prolonged a one perhaps, abruptly broken by the sound of the rain beating against the French door leading onto the terrace. I have lowered my eyes, and in the space that separates his dull black boots from my toes peeking out of my sandals, I seem to see a castle with paper walls rising in the air, or rather, a castle made of papers stuck together like bricks and full of words and deletions in my very own hand. It grows bigger and bigger, taller and taller. It is going to tumble down at the slightest sound, and I take refuge inside it, with my head hidden between my arms. I don't dare look out. In the lower part, forming the draw-bridge, I recognize some of the papers that I kept in the tin chest, fragments of my first diaries, poems, and little notes that a friend of mind at the Institute and I once passed each other from desk to desk — the first close friend I ever had. The mark of the folds in them is proof of how long ago they were written, even though they appear to be flattened out and glued to a piece of cardboard, forming a sort of collage. Her handwriting is bigger and more steady than mine, with the *a*'s firmly closed. No other girl had handwriting like that, bold and rebellious, as she herself was. She never lowered her head when she said that her parents, who were schoolteachers, were in prison because they were Reds. She looked straight ahead, proudly, afraid of nothing. We used to walk together to the outskirts of the city, down by the river or along the highway to Zamora, to catch insects for the Natural Sciences collection, and she would catch them with her hand, she even caught a cockroach in the kitchen once, and as she watched it kicking its legs in the air, she said it was very pretty. ("Aren't you scared of it?" I asked. "No, why should I be? It's not doing anybody any harm.") She was never scared or cold, the two all-enveloping sensations of those years that I remember: fear and cold clinging to one's body—"don't breathe a word about this," "beware of that," "don't go outside now," "pull your muffler up closer around your neck," "don't tell anybody they've killed Uncle Joaquín," "three degrees below freezing"—everybody was afraid, everybody talked about the cold. The winters of those war years were particularly severe and long: snow, ice, frost.

Volverá a reír la primavera
*que por cielo, tierra y mar se espera . . .**

The Falangists thundered that refrain in the streets, but spring was long in coming; the Institute was an inhospitable

*Spring will smile again / We await its coming, on land, at sea, and in the air
. . . (*Translator's note.*)

old mansion, without heating. She never wore a muffler. We came out of school in twilights with purplish clouds, eating our afternoon snacks of bread with chocolate. We had invented a desert island called Bergai. In those diaries of ours there is a map of the island and they recount the adventures we had on it. There must also be bits and pieces of a romantic novel that the two of us were writing together, though we never managed to finish it. The heroine's name was Esmeralda. She ran away from home one night because her parents were too rich and she wanted to have the adventure of living in the open air. She met, at the edge of a cliff, a stranger dressed in black standing with his back to her gazing at the sea.

"How old were you when you began to write?" the man in black asks me.

I look at him. He must be a mind reader. It's certain that he is. I don't know how, but he's seen the paper castle.

"Do you mean how old was I when I began to take refuge?"

He looks me straight in the eye, smiling. He's aware of what I'm thinking, of course. He knows everything.

"Yes, that's what I meant."

"A long time ago, during the war, in Salamanca."

"And what was it you were taking refuge from?"

"From the cold, I suppose. Or the bombings."

Drowning out the sound of the rain, the sirens warning of a bombing have begun to sound. That vibration, that suddenly shook the provinicial public square, pitilessly assaults the lofty battlements of the castle built of bits and pieces of my research on the eighteenth century, sets the entire edifice to tottering, and causes it to come crashing down. Left lying on top of the scattered papers is a large index card written in my handwriting of today (naturally: what is most recent always ends up on top) headed, in capital letters: "SIEGE OF MONTJUIC—1706—PHILIP V IS FORCED TO RETREAT," and underneath, in small letters, the description of that catastrophe. I remember that I wrote it in the Simancas archives, one sunny afternoon, after I had begun to take refuge in history, in dates. They raised camp during the night, all the artillery, baggage, provisions were abandoned, and the troops, harried by the enemy, fled through narrow defiles and gorges: ". . . to make matters still worse, the following day there was an eclipse of the sun and the panic grew." The paper sky has fallen and pinned me down, the soldiers of the Archduke Carlos run across my body. They are about to crush me. I wrap myself in the tattered standards, I am smothering to death, I must go seek another refuge, none of them is safe.

"Do you remember the bombings during the war?"

I look at the man in black without understanding at first which war he is referring to, that of the Succession or that of the year 1936.

"The bombings? Yes, of course I remember. One day a bomb fell in a cruller shop on the Calle Pérez Pujol, near home. The cruller seller's whole family was killed. The daughter was very nice, she played with us in the little square. Her father didn't like to go to the shelter, he said he preferred to die at home, that God's will is God's will. You see: that man lived in the open, he wasn't afraid."

"And how about you?"

"I wasn't afraid in those days either, because I didn't understand anything that was going on. Everything that was happening seemed so unreal to me. Go to the shelter? That was all right with me, it was just another game, a game invented by big people, but the rules of it were easy: as soon as you hear the siren, start running. Why? Nobody knew and nobody asked, it didn't matter, everybody simply obeyed the rules of the game. That cruller seller had refused to play and people thought he was crazy; poor man, he made wonderful crullers."

"Were there many shelters in Salamanca?"

"Lots of them. They sprang up like mushrooms in just a few months. They blocked the streets.

A tapar la calle, que no pase nadie,
que pasen mis abuelos, comiendo buñuelos . . .*

The cruller seller's daughter sang as we held hands. Her parents stopped making crullers and she stopped singing; they remained as examples of folly, as a reminder of how indispensable it was to have one's fear-alarm set all the time."

"And you went to the shelter?"

"What else could I have done, may I ask? . . ."

"Didn't you hear the siren?" My father appears in the doorway of his study, trying his best to appear calm. "Where are the girls?" My mother hurries down the hallway, calling us. We were cutting out paper dolls in the back room, a room that

---

*Block the street, don't let anybody through / just my grandma and grandpa, eating crullers . . . *(Translator's note.)*

had a green sofa with the bottom broken out and a chestnut-wood sideboard that is now in the kitchen here in this apartment. It was our playroom and classroom, but shortly thereafter, when there began to be shortages of everything, it was turned into a storeroom. We dropped the scissors and the pieces of cardboard. "Let's go to the shelter!" We went out to the stairway and ran into our third-floor neighbor, a very nervous army major, with a mustache like Ronald Colman's, who kept shouting as he dashed downstairs to the outside door: "Don't rush, all of you, there's no need to rush!" His family came down the stairs a little way behind him. One of his sons was my age. He smiled at me, took me by the hand: "Don't be afraid." We all crossed the Plaza de los Bandos beneath the insistent wail of the siren. The shelter was opposite. They had set it up by making use of a back street between the Iglesia del Carmen and Doña María la Brava's house. We entered it along with a crowd of people who came hurrying in helter-skelter and pushed us toward the back. My father tried to keep from being pushed farther back, stopped where he was, and looked around for us. "Let's see if we can't stay right here. Come on over here, don't get separated." They closed the doors and there wasn't room for one person more. "This is unbearable!" the big people said, packed together like sardines in this low, narrow vault. "A person can't breathe." And some of the children were crying, but I didn't have the slightest feeling of claustrophobia as long as the major's son kept hold of my hand. He protected me more than my parents. There was no comparison. "This is really cozy, isn't it?" he said in my ear. And we looked at each other, in each other's arms almost, taking advantage of the exceptional situation, squatting on our heels sometimes, so as to enjoy the feeling that we were all by ourselves down there in the midst of people's legs. "You must come upstairs to our place. Papa brought home some more saints yesterday. One of them is just beautiful, with a gold tunic. His name is San Froilán. He's so tall he hardly fits in the hallway." His father used to go out at night in a truck every so often to "requisition" treasures that had been left at the mercy of the first passerby inside abandoned churches in towns that had been taken by Nationalist troops. He would come back by night too and unload his booty. He kept going back and forth to the front, each time for the same reason. That third-floor hallway that looked like a museum fascinated me, but they didn't like people to come upstairs to their place. "I'll call to you from the patio in the afternoon, shall I, when Lucinda's the only one around?" Lucinda was a red-headed maid of theirs who watched over our affair of the heart, the sort of furtive love affair that ten-year-olds have. That boy and the daughter of the schoolteachers who were in prison were the first persons with whom I ever talked in secret. I wove tales and shared fantasies with each of them that I still remember, and I was equally fond of both of them, but I never spoke to either of them about the other because I had intuited that the two of them were never going to be able to love each other dearly, and the saddest part was that I didn't understand why. It was then that I discovered the heartbreak of irreconcilable passions, something I've experienced so many times since.

"The Nationalist General Headquarters was in Salamanca, wasn't it?"

"Yes, that's right, in the Palacio del Obispo."

"You must have seen Franco then."

"Of course I saw him. Once, I remember, after some ceremony or other in the cathedral, he was no farther away than from here to that table. He was very rigid, holding himself ramrod-straight in his leggings and his general's sash, waving and trying his best to look arrogant, though he always had a little potbelly. He was with his wife and daughter. They had only a small escort. It was the first time it ever occurred to me how dull life must be for the children of kings and ministers, because Carmencita Franco was looking around with a sad, utterly bored expression in her eyes. Our gaze met. She was wearing seed-stitch crocheted socks and patent-leather maryjanes. I thought to myself: what games does she play and who does she play them with? Her image remained engraved upon my memory forever. She was more or less my age, and people used to say she looked a little bit like me."

I feel the appraising gaze of my conversational partner fixed upon me.

"Like you?" he says. "What nonsense!"

I don't know whether to take this as a compliment or a dash of cold water. Carmencita Franco struck me as being very pretty, my taste, of course, being conditioned by everybody else's. The canons of taste, which vary so much from one era to another, are always related to the faces and styles of celebrities, those who for one reason or another have merited having their pictures in the papers. Another model for the adolescents of those days was Deanna Durbin, and curiously enough, even today I continue to associate the names of those two child-women in my mind, although at the time I felt them to be poles apart. Influenced by my reading of romantic novels, which used to place tearful stress on the dissatisfactions of rich heiresses, I thought of Franco's daughter as a creature trapped in a prison and under an evil spell, and I pitied her so much that I would even have liked to know her so as to be able to console her. I was reminded of the lines by Rubén Darío that I had learned by heart:

La princesa está triste
qué tendrá la princesa? *

So near and yet so far, shut up all day in the Palacio del Obispo, while I read stories by Antoniorrobles or cut castles out of cardboard in the back room that was so topsy-turvy and so cozy, and I paused to imagine her bored face looking at the same clouds that I was looking at just then:

. . . los suspiros se escapan de su boca de fresa
que ha peridido la risa, que ha perdido el color. †

Deanna Durbin, on the other hand, provided exemplary patterns of American behavior. I imagined her to be endowed with the same cleverness, daring, and resourcefulness that she displayed on screen in getting out of all the tight spots that the plots of her films kept getting her into. I had read that before she became an actress she rollerskated to school, with

---

*The princess is sad / What can be troubling the princess? *(Translator's note.)*
†. . . the sighs that escape her strawberry mouth / that has lost its laughter, lost its color. *(Translator's note.)*

her briefcase slung over her shoulder and—more difficult still!—eating a lemon ice-cream cone the while. I was fascinated by that image and kept pestering my parents till they finally bought me a pair of skates, but my mastery of that art never progressed beyond a dull mediocrity. I kept continually tripping and falling. How could I ever have dreamed of skating all the way to the Institute? To me that adventure represented the very image of freedom. I collected colored pictures of Deanna Durbin. They came in the weighing machines in pharmacies or with chocolate bars, little maroon and sepia photos on stiff cardboard, along with those of Claudette Colbert, Gary Cooper, Norma Shearer, Clark Gable, Merle Oberon, Paulette Goddard, Shirley Temple, intangible idols possessed of a mysterious, remote radiance. Franco's daughter too undoubtedly collected them, all by herself, with no brothers or sisters, amid the tapestries lining her gilded cage.

"Did you envy Carmencita Franco? my interviewer unexpectedly asks.

For the first time since he has entered the apartment, I am reminded that he is an interviewer, and I look at him with a sort of astonishment mingled with a sudden friendly warmth toward him. He doesn't have a tape recorder with him, he hasn't taken out a notebook to write anything down in it, nor has he asked me, as yet, any of the questions that are *de rigueur* among professional interviewers, so that he's drawn me out and encouraged me to pay him back in the same coin: there is no reason why my answers should be conventional either.

"Well, yes, I envied her a little on account of her hair," I say, "the way I envied Deanna Durbin. According to the reigning standards of fashion in those days, curly hair was the ideal, and mine was as straight as a string."

"And how did you wear it? In braids?"

"No, I had short hair. My mother curled it, by a very simple method that she had learned when she was little, putting it up in paper. It had become a ritual for her to put it up for me every night, and then later she showed me how, and it was like freeing myself from the maternal womb. I regarded myself as having come of age, as being really grown up, but it took a long time. I was already twenty years old by then, it was when I got that scholarship to Portugal that I told you about. It was indispensable to know how to put my hair up in paper curlers, I couldn't go through life with such straight hair."

"Why not? What about Greta Garbo?"

"Well, Greta Garbo didn't really go through life, strictly speaking. She floated through the ether instead. She was the exception, she was so off-beat, so far beyond the ordinary that she wasn't someone who set patterns. Who was going to dare imitate Greta Garbo? She was so unreal. And besides, her films, except for *Ninotchka,* had come out quite a bit earlier. The one who really first brazenly defied the curly-hair rule was Veronica Lake in *I Married a Witch.* And then there was Ingrid Bergman too, and here in Spain Ana Mariscal to a certain extent. But in any event those were isolated breaches of the convention, and straight hair continued to be held in disrepute all during the forties. I remember that when they gave the first Nadal Prize to a woman what impressed me as most revolutionary, apart from the despairing, nihilistic tone that she inaugurated with her novel, was her picture on the book jacket, with those short, straight locks of hers. I felt great twinges of envy, but at the same time a spark of hope, though in those days I was dreaming more of becoming an actress. I was in my first year at the university, and we were rehearsing several of Cervantes' one-act farces for a performance at the Teatro Liceo."

"And did you still go on putting your hair up in paper curlers?"

"Well, in '53, when I got married, my mother advised me to get myself a nice loose permanent. Up until that time, in Salamanca at least, permanents were mostly something that maidservants gave themselves, and the result was a head of hair like a blackamoor's, so kinky you couldn't even drag a comb through it. But by then we'd moved to Madrid and there were beauty salons and better methods. My mother thought it was a bad idea for me to put my hair up in paper curlers at night once I was married, you see, so I finally gave in, but that was the first and last permanent I've ever had in my life, and I cursed all beauty shops for all eternity. There were many fewer beauty shops in my childhood and my teens. Fixing one's hair, like cooking and dressmaking, was something done at home, and to a certain extent something personal and secret. Women used to curl their hair with curling irons or with tin curlers of various shapes and sizes, and then, with the plastics boom, rollers came along. But there's nothing, absolutely nothing, like paper curlers. I still use them sometimes. They don't split the ends of your hair or scorch it or keep you from sleeping."

"And how do you fasten them?"

"It's very simple—with a little twist when you get to the top."

"But they'd fall off."

"No, of course not, they stay in place very well. You usually cut toilet paper in strips to make them, you separate a lock of your hair and wind it up in the paper as though you were rolling a cigarette. The secret is not to let the ends get away, to catch them up securely. And then there's nothing to it, when you get to the top you twist the two ends of the paper together. Do you see what the wrapper of an almond wafer or a caramel looks like? Well, when you've put up a lock of your hair it looks like that and then you knot the two ends together."

I've ended up with my arms in the air and a lock of hair rolled up in my fingers. The man has followed, with an amused expression on his face, the gestures illustrating my explanation, which was perhaps too detailed, but the fact is that I'm not very dexterous, and what's more, he's drawn me out with all his questions. He continues to look at my hair, as though he were not at all inclined to change the subject. Is he going to ask me to give him a practical demonstration?

"Well," I say with a certain modesty, "it took me quite a while, as I've already told you, to learn to put my hair up in paper curlers by myself. Don't get the idea that it's all that easy."

"No, no, I realize that now. And what about Carmencita Franco?"

"Carmencita Franco? What about her?"

"I was wondering how she wore her hair."

"Ah, I see! She wore it short too."

"There you are. And to your way of thinking she never put it up in paper curlers?"

I look at him. He has planted a doubt in my mind, but it's one that is altogether too disturbing.

"No, no," I finally say, banishing the very thought, "it was naturally curly. It was easy to tell the difference between naturally curly hair and the other kind."

"And there was nothing else you envied her for?"

A silence falls. I search my memory, in exhaustive detail, as I did when I was a little girl before going to confession.

"No, truly not, that was the one thing I envied her for. On the contrary, I felt sorry for her, if you want the real truth of the matter. Besides, people in my family weren't Francophiles."

I see him put his hand in his pocket and I heave a sigh, regretting having mentioned politics. He is surely going to take out a notebook and a ball-point pen to make notes on the ideology that ruled my upbringing. Heaven help me, he's wearied of all these digressions. But what he takes out of his pocket, from a king-sized pack, is a slender brown cigarillo, which he raises to his mouth.

"Would you like one?" he asks then, holding the pack out to me. "They're Portuguese."

I smile in relief as I take one. I look at it.

"Portuguese you say? Oh, yes, they called them 'cheroots.'"

"We can smoke one in homage to that young man from Coimbra and your emancipation. What do you say?"

"Very well, better late than never. I didn't smoke back in those days, there were almost no girls from the provinces who did; people thoroughly disapproved."

"Not even Carmencita Franco?"

I shrug. The yellow wick of his lighter flares, he offers me a light and then lights up himself. The very first puff leaves a strong, biting taste on my tongue. What a pleasure. We can go on talking about everything and nothing.

"In other words, you thought of yourself as being happier than Franco's daughter," he says.

I hesitate for a few seconds before answering. I could tell him that happiness in the war years and the years just after the war was something inconceivable, that we lived surrounded by ignorance and repression. I could tell him about those textbooks with all sorts of things missing that kept us from getting a decent education, about the friends of my parents put to death by a firing squad or driven into exile, about Unamuno, about military censorship, and add the bitterness of my present opinions to the other sensations that I am dredging up from my memory tonight, like an unexpected odor that comes in waves. I almost never capture them like this, in their pure, pristine state, just as they arise spontaneously. I force them, rather, to change direction, so that they remain focused beneath the light of an interpretation after the fact that masks the memory. Nothing would be easier than to resort to such distortion, since it has become so habitual in this sort of conversation. But this man does not deserve stereotyped responses.

"The truth of the matter is that I remember my childhood and my adolescence, despite everything, as a very happy time in my life. The mere fact of buying a five-centavo ice cream, the sort that the street vendor spread between two wafers with a silver-plated paddle, was a real treat. Perhaps because we were hardly ever given money, we got a great deal of pleasure out of the little we had. I remember the pleasure of sucking the ice cream very slowly so it would last."

My reply doesn't seem to come as any great shock to him. The only question he asks is:

"Were they good?"

"Excellent, especially the lemon ones."

I don't know if it is because of the memory of the ice-cream sandwiches that, incidentally, I always savored remembering Deanna Durbin, or the bite of the dark brown cigarillo, but the fact remains that I am suddenly aware that my mouth is very dry and that I'm terribly thirsty.

"Excuse me, aren't you thirsty?"

"Yes, a little," he admits.

I haven't offered him anything to drink yet and I would like to detain him, though in all truth he has given no sign of being in a hurry and hasn't once glanced at his watch. But it may well be that he isn't wearing a watch.

"Do you like tea?"

"Yes, very much."

"It's iced tea, with lemon. I make it in the morning, and put it in a thermos with little pieces of ice."

"It's the very best thirst-quencher," he says. "I used to make it too once upon a time."

"Well, wait a moment. I'm going to go get some in the kitchen."

I rise to my feet, and as I head down the hall, I hear his voice at my back saying:

"Watch out for cockroaches!"

COME TO CÚNIĜAN SOON

I'M IN A good mood as I enter the kitchen. I turn on the light: the cockroach isn't there. Before hunting up the thermos, I begin picking up the remains of a snack still lying on the table, carry the dirty dishes over to the sink, and then wipe the checkered oilcloth with a damp rag.

I note an incentive that I've been lacking for months. A little order is the first thing necessary to make solitude hospitable. I'll set to work tomorrow to go over my papers and clean out my files. The conversation with this man has stimulated me and breathed new life into my old subject of romantic rituals in the postwar era. Two years ago I began to take notes for a book that I thought I might give that title to, more or less the world of my *Peeking Through the Curtains,* but explored now, with greater distance, in something like an essay or memoirs, I don't really know, what I still don't have any idea of is what form I could cast it in. I organized all my material for it by subject: dressmakers, beauty shops, songs, dances, novels, mores, turns of speech, bars, movies, setting it all down in a notebook with green and blue covers that I began immediately after Franco's death. Incidentally, I wonder what's happened to that notebook? The thought that I might have lost it upsets me. But I'm not going to allow myself to be obsessed by it. I'll look for it after a while. Right now I have something better to do: offering tea to this stranger so that a conversation that is doing me so much good won't die. I feel like calling to him to come see the kitchen, just because it would cheer me up to hear him say that it's a cozy room, to spy the reflection of these worn surfaces and these dark tones that his eyes would beam back to me. I have a horror of today's aseptic, luxurious, impersonal kitchens, where nobody would sit down to chat, those precincts ruled by the worship of ventilating fans, garbage disposals, dishwashers, by the stereotyped smile of the housewife, carefully and skillfully copied from that of television models, that woman obliged by propaganda to make being merely "well-organized" a goal and a great victory, incapable of any sort of relation with the ever-changing, latest-model equipment and machines that her spotless hands manipulate. I think of the interiors of Vermeer of Delft: the charm of a painting of his lies in the symbiosis that he managed to capture between the woman who is reading a letter or looking out the window and the everyday utensils that serve her as silent company, the relationship of the human figure and those well-worn pieces of furniture that surround her like a reminder of her childhood. There is no reason to be so afraid of the mark of time.

I have finished cleaning off the oilcloth table cover. I raise my eyes and see myself reflected with a hopeful, cheerful expression in the mirror with an antique frame hanging on the wall to the right, above the maroon sofa. There is just a touch of mockery in the reflected smile on noting that I am carrying a dustcloth in my hand. To tell the truth, the girl who is looking back at me is a child of nine and then a youngster of eighteen, standing in the huge dining room of my grandparents' apartment in the Calle Mayor in Madrid, come back to life from the depths of the mirror—was it this same mirror? She is about to raise one finger and point it at me: "Well, well, you're cleaning, I never thought I'd live to see the day." She has appeared to me at other times when I least expected it, like a wise and providential ghost, in twenty-four years she has never tired of keeping watch over me so as to put me on my guard against the dangers lurking in domestic life, and she always emerges from the same place, from that imposing dining room, from the mirror that hung over the fireplace. I usually put her mind at rest and we end up laughing together. "Thanks, my girl, but don't worry, really I'm the same as always, I haven't let myself be brainwashed." Much more than in my house in Salamanca, or in the summerhouse in Galicia, it was in that apartment in Madrid, when we came on vacation during Easter Week or Christmas, that my schemes for disobeying the laws of the household were hatched and my first rebellions against order and cleanliness took place—two different notions and one true god to whom worship must be paid, invisibly enthroned alongside the images of Saint Joseph and the Virgin of Perpetual Help, in every corner of that fourth-floor apartment on the right at No. 14, Calle Mayor, a convent run by my grandmother with the help of two ancient servants, an aunt and a niece, who had been born in the province of Burgos.

I recently passed by that building with a friend. Everything is exactly the same: the balconies with hoops along them for flowerpots and the wrought-iron dividers between the rooms leading off them. I stopped on the sidewalk opposite —"those balconies on the right, the ones on the fourth floor." I told my friend how they used to put out hangings when parades and processions passed by and how they tied the crinkly Palm Sunday frond to the railing. I remember how it then began to get dustier and dustier and duller and duller. I ran my eyes down the façade. The bakery shop is still next to the downstairs door. When my father was in law school this district was right in the center of Madrid and the king and queen passed by on their way to the Palacio de Oriente, but now it has lost its majestic air. I stood there looking inside the dark doorway, wondering if the elevator had been repaired. It went upstairs through an iron cage and you could hear it creak in every single room in the building, like a woodborer working intermittently. It used to stop most often at the *pension* on the third floor, "The Pearl of Galicia," from which there came up via the inner courtyard the sound of young guests, who sometimes appeared in shirt-sleeves. I would raise my head from my book, listening for the iron door of the elevator slamming shut—"it's stopped on the third floor again." Nothing, there was no one coming up to our floor. No unexpected visitor ever rang our doorbell, the sort of visitor I conjured up in dreams, bestowing on him the face of people I had happened to see on the street whose lives I knew intuitively involved some extraordinary, exciting tale. For school compositions, I wrote a number of variations on this theme of the unexpected visit, and some of them didn't turn out badly at all; from that time on I've come to associate literature with breaches of habit. Sometimes, in the afternoon, people, inevitably the same ones, came to the house, old friends of my parents and grandparents who always telephoned before coming by, whose visits were a lifeless ritual, who never had anything surprising to say, and whom we were obliged to smile at if they asked us about our studies or remarked how we'd grown. They would be received in the dining room, and would sit down in the big green velvet armchairs next to the fireplace, and time would begin to bounce back and forth against the walls, a restless prisoner. It didn't make any noise, but I could feel it throbbing from where I was sitting at the big table with the thick felt cover, quite a long way away from them, for the room was huge. I couldn't see why children had to "come out and be with the visitors," but it was tacitly understood that that was how it would be. We would be told that Señor and Señora So-and-So would be coming, that they were very anxious to see us. But once they had arrived nothing about their attitude made such an assertion seem at all likely to me. I would put the black lead earphones on. They were broadcasting a foxtrot:

Un novio le ha salido a Socorrito,
la mar de rebonito,
un joven ideal.

Se ondula, juega al tennis, bebe soda,
y sólo con la Kodak
*se gasta un dineral . . .**

If I took them off, I could hear that the conversation next to the fireplace was still meandering along, the principal subjects being health, food, and family. It was like a fog descending. I looked at the dim outlines of their faces and gave them a pale smile from time to time. It was bad manners to keep to myself like that. I began to draw, to make paper dolls from the illustrations in old fashion magazines or paste decals in an album with my head bent over the felt cloth. I was protected by the disorder of the pencils, pencil sharpeners, scissors scattered all over the felt, objects that became friends through being used and being allowed their freedom, that recovered their identity on ceasing "to be in their right place." And the green light of the lamp slid down the back of my neck like cherry jam, as from the kitchen or the bedrooms there came the muffled bustling to and fro of the two maidservants who had known my father as a child and ever since had been tirelessly cleaning, pots and pans, tile floors, door handles, moldings, endlessly cleaning. The tumultuous city outside was an invitation to adventure. It was calling to me. My whole body was an antenna straining to catch the rattling of the yellow streetcars, the echo of the car horns, the gleam of the electric signs enlivening the Puerta del Sol, out there just a few steps away, and I felt as

*Socorrito has gotten herself a sweetheart, / he's terribly good-looking, / an ideal young man. / He marcels his hair, plays tennis, drinks soda, / and spends a fortune on his Kodak alone . . . *(Translator's note.)*

though I had been swallowed up by a whale. What came to my ears was the great gaping yawn of the house with its unbearable ticktocking clocks and its inert gleaming silver and porcelain, a temple of order, supported by invisible columns of clean linen, ironed and put away inside chests of drawers, table and bed linen, embroidered runners, starched shirts, bedspreads, needlework insertions, lace, faggoting. I wanted to begin opening up drawers and chests and spattering ink all over that oppressive inheritance from industrious great-grandmothers, but I just sat there with my head bent over the table cover, making prim and proper drawings: a little girl walking through the forest with her basket, a family having dinner, a man peering out of the little window of a train, a woman lying in bed. "Almost anything keeps that one amused," my mother was saying. "She likes studying so much." "Too much," my grandmother was saying. "Heaven only knows why she spends so much of her time thinking." The mirror above the fireplace reflected my curly hair that had been put up in strips of paper. I painted a head with curly hair surrounded by draperies, vases, plaster statues, would there ever be any way out of that narrow passage? Where could Cúnigan be?

I had a very vague idea of Cúnigan. To tell the truth, I never even managed to find out if it was a place that really existed, and the only things I knew about it I'd learned from a little ditty that seemed more like a singing commercial. I'd heard it only once or twice on the radio, or maybe I only dreamed that I'd heard it, because other people laughed when they heard me humming it and asked me where in the world I'd picked up such a silly song. It went:

Ven pronto a Cúnigan,
si no has estado en Cúnigan,
lo encontraras espléndido,
mágico,
único,
magnífico en verdad.
¿Dónde vas a merendar?
Voy a Cúnigan, Cúnigan, Cúnigan.
Por las noches ¿dónde vas?
*Voy a Cúnigan a bailar.**

Obviously Cúnigan was a unique, magic place, and most likely it really did exist. With a little luck one could find it somewhere in the labyrinth of streets and signs that made up the map of Madrid. It didn't matter to me that I lacked concrete clues. My very special magic powers, my desire were all I needed, but the great obstacle was the lack of freedom. That sort of search had to be embarked upon all by oneself and certain risks were involved. If I was never left by myself it was useless to even try to find it.

When I went out on the streets in Madrid, it was always with my parents to carry out in their company a program of activities that I had had no hand in planning, and as we finished each one my father would cross it off the list in his memorandum book. It was a program all laid out before starting

*Come to Cúnigan soon, / if you've never been to Cúnigan, / you'll find it's marvelous, / magic, / unique, / really magnificent. / Where do you go to have lunch? / I go to Cúnigan, Cúnigan, Cúnigan. / Where do you go at night? / I go to Cúnigan to dance. *(Translator's note.)*

out on the journey, a cherished plan they had worked out during long winter evenings in front of the fire, with a methodical and minutely detailed sense of expectation that they tried their best to communicate to my sister and me, with fair success at times, since the very name of the capital, called to mind in the provinces, by the light of a lamp, unfailingly cast its wondrous spell, no matter what the plan might be. "That'll be for when we go to Madrid. We'll do better in Madrid." Everything that needed to be bought, seen, or consulted was left till the coming trip. It wouldn't be long now. We lived on that deceptive sense of keen anticipation.

One came to Madrid, first and foremost, to go to the dressmaker's. Until about twenty years ago, when mass production began to back into a corner those skilled at making clothes to order by hand, acquiring a wardrobe was a slow and enjoyable business, guided by various rituals requiring practice and an apprenticeship that occupied a large part of women's time and a large part of their conversations with their lady friends and their husbands. There was a sewing machine in every house and there were always fashion books all about that someone was consulting, not idly leafing through them, but conscientiously studying them, trying to figure out the complicated puzzle of how all those gathers, gussets, bias piping, ruffles, tucks, and smocking shown in the sketch fitted together. "Yes, of course, it all looks very nice the way it's pictured there, but this fabric is too thick, I don't know what it will look like when it's made up." "That's no dress for Doña Petra to make for you, of course, Doña Petra would botch it." Dressmakers were divided into two main categories: those who gave one reason to fear that they might botch a dress, and those who never botched one. Naturally this classification, being subjective, depended on the degree of reliability that the customer attributed to the one who was going to be entrusted with doing the work, and in view of the fact that the "botching" of a dress — even though it was a question of an absolutely personal judgment — eventually became a subject of public gossip, the individual loss of faith in a certain dressmaker immediately gave rise to a lack of confidence in her on the part of other possible customers who had heard talk of her failure. The news that slipshod work had been done was passed on mercilessly, the redemption of the guilty party was put in question, suspicion spread, and the sum of these multiple losses of confidence sooner or later resulted in a loss of status. Those dressmakers who had the reputation of having botched dresses on more than one occasion were most likely demoted for life to the rank of mere seamstresses. "Well, what can you expect of Doña Petra, poor thing, everyone knows she's not a dressmaker, she's a seamstress." Seamstresses, who customarily alternated working in their own homes and working by the day, for miserable pay, in other people's households, were preferably entrusted only with bathrobes, everyday skirts, undergarments, maids' uniforms, and children's clothes. Some of them, already advanced in years, "seamstresses all their lives," lived in modest apartments on bottom floors, without a plaque on the door, and in the dark bedroom where they took our measurements and had us try on the garments, they usually had a bed with different-colored cushions amid which lay a china doll with dusty hair and little satin slippers. When they came to sew at people's houses, they would bring sweets or caramels for the children, tell them stories, and give them the empty spools and snippets of cloth from the work at hand that had been left lying on the floor of the sewing room, where, after the seamstress had gone, a characteristic odor lingered on. Moreover, they were treated with a mixture of condescension and familiarity, and people put them to all sorts of trouble, demanding that they make endless adjustments and alterations. As a general rule their extraordinary patience was matched by their total lack of ambition.

Dressmakers properly speaking, that is to say those who had had the good luck to earn themselves a reputation as such, never came to other people's houses, and their relative standing was based on the luxury with which they had set themselves up in business and the slowness with which they delivered the work entrusted to them. The fact that their prestige varied in inverse proportion to the promptness with which they finished work and never in direct proportion always surprised me. "She's really very good, but she's very slow, she won't have it ready for you till after Christmas," people used to say, this being the highest possible recommendation. Those who had the best reputations were, naturally, the most expensive ones, and furthermore they had a great many illustrated fashion magazines, some of them from abroad. They consulted them with the customer in the fitting room and allowed themselves to offer suggestions and advice as to how the garment should be made. But it was always the customer who bought the material. In the provinces there simply were no dressmakers who would not allow customers to bring their own material. The title of titles, that of a dressmaker who provides the material herself, was flaunted only by a handful of modistes in Madrid.

The visit to one of these Madrid modistes, whose name was Lúcia, Amalia's daughter, and who lived in the Calle de Goya, constituted one of the indispensable milestones of our stay in the capital, whether we went to her establishment to place a definite order or simply to see her spring-summer or autumn-winter collections. She was a slender, elegant woman with very thin eyebrows, who had made my mother's trousseau when she was married. I inherited one of the dresses in it, of royal purple crepe trimmed in gray silk, and I still sometimes wear it. She received us graciously, by appointment, invited us to be seated in the little chairs of an anteroom full of oval mirrors, showed us samples of fabrics, and shortly thereafter a sister of hers, who looked quite a bit like her, modeled the dresses in the collection for the four of us. My most striking impression of that parade of costumes was the abrupt transformation of Lúcia's sister into a mute and distant mannequin, when a few minutes before she had greeted us and kissed us with a great show of affection. I watched her pirouetting in front of us with those successive shoulder capes and filmy dresses, towering over us in her high heels, stopping dead still, walking over to us so that my mother could appreciate the quality of the fabric, staring into space as though she didn't know us or had really turned into a wind-up doll. When the showing ended and we were about to leave, she would come out to join her sister and bid us goodbye at the door.

Another of the fundamental objectives of the trip to Madrid was going to see first-run films or new plays that hadn't yet come to the provinces.

Going to the theater was a much more solemn and exceptional occasion than going to the movies. Sooner or later the first-run films came to Salamanca and they were the same films, exactly the same. Theater companies, on the other hand, came only during the September holidays, and though their repertory included some of the successes of the Madrid season, the performances were completely different, the stage settings were much less elaborate, and the actors did little more than walk through their roles. Of all the things we did in Madrid, what I liked most was going to the theater. My father bought the tickets in advance, and sometimes families my parents knew were invited to go with us, in which case we often rented an orchestra stall. When the usher opened the door of the enclosure with his key, handed my parents the program, and stepped aside to let us past, I felt as though I were entering a privileged tabernacle. No landscape in the world, no religious ceremony, no parade could arouse such emotion in me as that I experienced on looking out over the orchestra seats illuminated by great crystal chandeliers and taking my place in the raised box with railings encased in velvet. Once inside it the performance began then and there, and my mother's gestures, slowly removing her gloves and taking out her opera glasses, seemed to me to be those of a great actress. But nothing could compare to the moment when the house lights went down, the whispers died away, and the curtain rose to transport us into a room we had never seen before, where characters who were strangers to us, about whom we knew nothing as yet, were about to tell us of their conflicts. Almost always one of them was already on-stage, reading the paper, sitting on a sofa, or gazing in silence at another character who was about to address him. Those first moments of silence brought a lump to my throat, I admired the actors for those pauses, for their poise as they waited. I wanted to be an actress when I grew up. I wanted to live hundreds of different lives. On returning home and listening to my parents' conversation at dinner those names, Loreto Prado, Antonio Vico, Irene López Heredia, or Concha Catalá, that graced their remarks sounded to me like the names of deities.

Besides going to the theater, to the movies, and visiting Lúcia, Amalia's daughter, we would also go to have an apéritif at some place just recently opened, to consult doctors, to visit the Prado Museum, to buy things in the big department stores, to do the Stations of the Cross on Holy Thursday, with the Blessed Sacrament exposed amid gleaming candles, to the Plaza Mayor to buy moss for the crèche at Christmastime, or to return one or another of those family visits which brought back the feeling of being trapped. Very often, I would linger behind looking at the sign on a street that seemed to lead elsewhere. "Come on, child! What are you looking at?" "Nothing, just that street there, why don't we go that way?" I envied the people entering narrow, unknown streets, perhaps heading for Cúnigan.

People in Madrid walked differently, looked at things, dressed, and talked differently, with a sort of swagger. I used to steal glances at the changing faces that, once in a very great while, would stare back into mine for a few instants, above all during rides on the Metro. Inside the subway car, where there was no need to seek pretexts for brushing up against other people's bodies and breathing in their odor, I liked the odor of those strangers who might be about to get off at the next station, whereupon I would be doomed to lose sight of them forever. I tried to decipher, from the expression on their faces and the cut of their clothes, what their occupation was or what they might be thinking about. Who knew whether one or another of them might be going to Cúnigan? If I got off behind them I could follow them, enter a street I didn't know, see what the door of the building that they were heading for looked like. Perhaps they were hastening to a secret rendezvous. It would be so easy, but in order to do that it was necessary to be able to go about by myself. Nothing could ever happen to me until I was able to go out on the streets alone. We got off at Sol, climbed up the stairs of the subway station, started walking: the Mallorquina pastry shop, the Cine Pleyel, the Camerana clothing store. Our door was already in sight. I swore to myself that I would never again walk down the Calle Mayor once I was able to go about the streets of Madrid by myself.

I hadn't walked down the Calle Mayor for some time, I told my friend as we stood there in front of the balconies of No. 14 the other afternoon, and then, as we walked on, I had the feeling that I was breaking the ties that bound me to that old façade. All of a sudden we were an anonymous couple walking down an anonymous street. I began to tell him stories of those days when I visited the capital as though peeking through a back door. He is younger than I am, he doesn't remember the yellow streetcars. He's never heard of Cúnigan in his life, nor ever seen Celia Gámez onstage. "If you wanted to write something about those years you wouldn't need to go to periodicals libraries," he said to me. We walked through one of the arches opening onto the Plaza Mayor. The old-fashioned hardware store, "El Relámpago: Floor Polish," was still on the corner. Night was falling and it seemed to me that I had crossed a line on the other side of which the world became mysterious, a zone where the unforeseen might happen and the persons spied from the balcony were now a shadow disappearing in the distance. "Where can that couple be going?" and I gaily began to sing "I'm going to Cúnigan, Cúnigan, Cúnigan," as disappointment dimmed the eyes bidding us goodbye and I felt the cold of the glass against my forehead as I stood on tiptoe watching from beneath the drawn curtain.

"That child and her mania for sitting and reading with her face glued to the balcony!" my grandmother used to complain. "Can't you see the marks that your fingers and your nose leave on the windowpanes? The windows that have just been cleaned, for goodness' sake!" But what was there that hadn't just been cleaned, just folded, just put away in its proper place? And why was it that the proper place of things couldn't be simply the one where they happened to be at a given moment? And above all, why punish them with that continuous, cruel purgative of having their dust removed, the way the scabs of a disease are forcibly pulled off? The dust descended in spirals in the rays of sunlight, landed silently on things. It was something so natural and so peaceful. I watched it settle with perverse delight. I felt like a secret ally of the brazen enemy, which, finding itself beset by implacable battues to rout it, redoubled its minuscule battalions to fight back with greater tenacity still. From early dawn on, the first ray of light that brought to my bed a fine rain of motes of dust coincided with the maid's diligent efforts to capture it, the fanatical orders from her superior as reveille blew, the deployment of equipment hidden in a dark closet in the hallway, and immediately thereafter that sweeping, scrubbing, and shaking of brooms, brushes, feather dusters, fur dusters, dustpans, squares of chamois, flannel cloths, dustmops. I had made common cause with the persecuted, I gave it secret orders and secret refuge, I offered it sanctuary in my bed. "Come on, hide yourself in here. Your vengeance is to make mock of them and be reborn somewhere else, they can't get the better of you." And when someone came into the room to tell me that it was breakfast time, I pretended I'd been fast asleep till just that minute.

Of the two maids from Burgos, the skinnier and younger one (though describing her as young is absurd since she was ageless) had as her principal duty keeping the house clean. She was the one responsible for sacking the bedrooms while the beds were still warm, for throwing the windows wide open, shaking the rugs, and scrupulously picking up the clothing scattered about. Meanwhile her aunt, a more imposing and authoritative figure, performed, as she served us our chocolate, another of the important solemn rites that marked the dawn of a new day and were her exclusive province: consulting us, before readying herself to go to the market, as to what we would like for lunch and dinner, a question which, at that hour of the day, as we sat confronting a copious breakfast, was very nearly impossible to answer with even a minimum of interest. But it was more impossible still to escape her stubborn interrogation, preceded by the enumeration of the different viands and their respective possibilities of preparation, with respect to which we were obliged to announce our gastronomic preferences. Her sensibilities were offended by the fact that her meticulous descriptions liberally interspersed with diminutives failed to rouse our gluttony, our gratitude, or our jubilation. I dreamed of living in a garret where clothes were never hung up and there were books strewn all over the floor, where nobody hunted down the flecks of dust drifing in the sunbeams, where one ate only when one was ravenously hungry, without further ado.

"Don't worry, my girl, I haven't changed as far as essentials are concerned, the only thing that gets attended to are absolutely necessary tasks, and meals are improvised on the spot. What gets put on the table is whatever there is on hand, with no frills and in a jiffy, simply to keep the conversation going. The important thing is to go on talking, with other people or with oneself. But you must understand also that every so often it's necessary to pick up a little so that the atmosphere continues to be inviting. It's necessary to compromise a bit. One ought not to worship disorder in and for itself either. All ironclad principles are bad. I'll tell you some other day what my present thoughts are on the subject of order and disorder. I've been here in this kitchen for twenty-four years now, my girl, so you can see I've had plenty of time to mull over this whole business of housekeeping, and I can assure you that too much disorder is depressing, it can even get to the point of making me not care if I live any longer or not, the way drug addicts end up. But of course you don't know anything about people like that, you never got any farther than Cúnigan. I'll tell you some other day, right now I'm in something of a hurry. I just came to get the thermos full of tea so that a conversation I was in the midst of in the room back there won't die. I have a visitor, see? An unexpected and rather strange visitor, by the way, like the ones in the compositions for school. You'd find him fascinating."

The thermos is behind me, on the sideboard: a huge sideboard with black moldings that is reflected in the mirror and occupies the entire wall opposite. It comes from my mother's side of the family. All of Galicia flows through it. For many years it was in Salamanca in the back room, where I learned to play and to read, activities presided over by this chestnut-wood ancestor, at once so stable and such a great traveler. Once upon a time it belonged to Don Javier Gaite, who bought it in Orense for three hundred pesetas, according to a bill that his daughter María, my mother, found not long ago among other papers. Old papers always have old stories that go along with them, and she tells them to me because she knows I like them. I never knew my grandfather, but in photographs of him he's very good-looking, with his little neatly trimmed black beard and intelligent eyes peeking out from underneath his panama hat. He never liked settling down for very long in any one place. Perhaps it's from him that I inherited just a touch of Bohemianism, though of a mild sort. He was a professor of geography and kept putting in for transfers, wandering from one provincial Institute to another and carting the sideboard around with him from one place to the next, so that it ended up in many towns and many houses. My mother remembers one in Cáceres especially, the place where they stayed the longest. It had any number of rooms and the rent was six duros. Recently, when I happened to mention to her that nowadays houses have very little mystery about them and all living rooms seem to be the same living room, she got to talking about those old houses and I asked her to draw me a plan of the one in Cáceres. In the beginning, it struck her as a silly whim of mine and she began to draw it rather reluctantly, just to please me, but then, as she drew each room and started having trouble with the proportions and the way they fitted together, she got all enthused and went to get graph paper so as to try to solve the problems, and finally we both got so interested we forgot to set the table for lunch, and I told her that good stories always make a person lose all sense of time and that thanks to them we keep ourselves from being overwhelmed by practical tasks, and that remark led to a really delightful chat. It was an enormous house, with a quite complicated layout, full of inside courtyards to let in light, narrow hallways, and odd corners. The dining room was in the back of the house and led onto an open gallery where my mother used to sit and read, because the weather was very pleasant in Cáceres. If she looked up, she saw a bright blue sky, with storks gliding above the rooftops. If she looked inside the house through the door, she saw that sideboard.

That dining room was also called "the back room," so that the two of us have each had our back room. I also imagine it as the attic of one's brain, a sort of secret place full of a vague jumble of all sorts of miscellaneous junk, separated from the cleaner and more orderly anterooms of the mind by a curtain that is only occasionally pulled back. The memories that may come to us as something of a surprise live in hiding in the back room. They always emerge from there, and only when they want to. It's no use trying to flush them out.

My mother spent her idle hours in the gallery off the back room, putting treasures in the little tin chest, and she can't decide if time went by quickly or slowly, nor is she able to say exactly how she divided it. All she knows is that she was never bored and that she read *The Three Musketeers* there. From the time she was just a little girl, she loved to read and to play children's games, and she would have liked to study at the university, like her two brothers, but it wasn't the custom in those days for girls to prepare for a career, so the thought never even crossed her mind to ask to do so. When I was studying for my bachelor's degree, she gave me a novel to read entitled *Love and the Professor,* the story of a girl who dares to go to the university, falls in love with her Latin professor, and eventually marries him. The ending disappointed me a little. I wasn't really convinced that that girl had done the right thing by marrying a man much older than herself and a monomaniac in the bargain, apart from which I also thought "she didn't need all those provisions for such a short trip," placing so many hopes in studying for a career and defying the society that prevented a woman from realizing those hopes, and then having it all turn out that way, the usual happy ending. Who could tell if it would have been all that happy, since sooner or later that girl was bound to feel disillusioned. Moreover, why did all novels have to end when people got married? I liked the whole process of falling in love, the obstacles, the tears and the misunderstandings, the kisses in the moonlight, but once the wedding had taken place there didn't seem to be anything more to tell. It was as though life itself had ended. Very few novels or films dared to go further and tell us what that love turned out to be like after the bride and groom vowed at the altar to love each other for all eternity, and to tell the truth that roused my suspicions. My mother was not the sort who was eager to see me married. She never taught me to cook, or to sew either, though I watched her closely when I saw her doing those things, and I think I learned how from watching her. On the other hand, she always encouraged me in my studies and when, after the war, my friends came to the house for cram-sessions at exam time, she brought us snacks and looked at us with envy in her eyes. "A clever person learns even such a thing as how to sew a button on better than a stupid one," she retorted one day when a lady, shaking her head in disapproval, had said of me, "A woman who knows Latin can come to no good end," and I looked at my mother in eternal gratitude.

In those days, I had enough sense to understand that the "bad end" which that proverb warned against had to do with the dark threat of remaining a spinster, implicit in all the tasks, teachings, and sermons of the Women's Section of the Falangist party. Rhetoric in the postwar era was devoted to discrediting the feminist stirrings that had begun in the years of the Republic, and stressed once again the unselfish heroism of wives and mothers, the importance of their silent and obscure labor as pillars of the Christian home and family. All the harangues that our instructors and female comrades subjected us to in those inhospitable buildings, reminiscent at once of airplane hangars and popular movie houses, where I grudgingly did my Social Service, sewing hems, doing gymnastics, and playing basketball, all turned out to have the same aim: to get us to accept, with pride and joy, with a steadfastness that nothing could discourage, as evidenced by sedate conduct that would never be clouded by the slightest shadow of slander, our status as strong women, the complement and mirror of the male. The two most important virtues were industriousness and happiness, and both were indissolubly combined in those pieces of practical advice which greatly resembled a sure-fire family recipe. Just as a cake could not fail to rise in the oven if eggs were beaten into flour and sugar in the recommended proportions, neither could there be any doubt as to the proper hardening of those two elements — happiness and activity — that were indispensable for shaping the upright woman, the Spanish wife. Carmen de Icaza, the literary spokeswoman of those ideals, in her most famous novel, *Cristina Guzmán,* which all girls of marriageable age read sitting on cots and many soldiers carried about in their knapsacks, had written; "Life smiles on the person who smiles on it, not on the one who makes faces at it." One was to smile as a matter of precept, not because one felt like it or ceased to feel like it. Her heroines were active and practical. They choked back their tears, confronted any and every calamity without a word of complaint, looking toward a future edged in pink clouds, invulnerable to the pernicious dejection that could seep in only through the cracks of indolence. In Falangist hymns, the nurse laughs joyfully after her day's work: "nurse of the new Spain dawning, no one can lure you away from your post at the bedside of those in pain." Pain was an insignificant and ridiculous cockroach. One needed only to keep all the corners of the house clean for it to flee in mortification, put to shame by its trivial existence. One needn't even deign to look at the alarming forms or shadows lurking in the dark. Optimistic women rose at dawn to open the windows and breathe deeply as they did calisthenics, keeping before their eyes, like an illustrated catechism manual to guide their respective movements, the series of drawings marked off in squares offered them each month for five pesetas in the pages of the magazine *Y*, published by the Women's Section. The *Y* of the title was topped with a crown that was an allusion to a certain glorious queen whose name began with that initial: *Adivina adivinanza, la fatiga no la alcanza, siempre en danza, desde el Pisuerga al Arlanza, con su caballo y su lanza.** It wasn't necessary to be particularly good at solving riddles, we all knew her only too well, we had heard her name only too often: it was Queen Isabella. We were placed beneath her advocacy, we were given talks about

---

*Guess the answer to this riddle, she's someone who's never weary, continually on the move, from the Pisuerga to the Arlanza, with her horse and her lance. (*Translator's note.*)

her iron will and her spirit of sacrifice, we were told how she had held the ambition and the despotism of the nobles in check, how she had created the Holy Office, expelled the traitorous Jews, given up her jewels to finance the most glorious undertaking in our history. Yet even so there had been those who had slandered her because of her fidelity to her ideals, those who had called her abnegation cruelty. I looked at that severe face, imprisoned in a helmet, that kept cropping up in the textbooks, and the only thing I didn't understand was the part about happiness. Perhaps it was just a bad portrait of her, but of course those textbooks didn't particularly inspire you to keep that image before you as a mirror, and of course some of the instructresses who urged us to imitate her also had their mouths set in that same rigid grin and had that same cold gleam in their eyes, even though they spoke continually of happiness. Happiness was a reward for having done one's duty and was the diametrical opposite of doubt. We were told about the ascent to the lofty peaks, above which imperial eagles soared and from which everything could be seen clearly. And likewise in the Advice to the Lovelorn column in Y, all the problems that might prey upon the soul of maladjusted or irresolute souls were banished with one stroke of the pen. All of them were solved by not sitting with folded hands, not wasting time. Queen Isabelle never gave herself a moment's respite, never doubted. Proud of her legacy, we would fulfill our mission as Spanish women, we would learn to make the sign of the cross on our children's foreheads, to air a room, to make use of every last scrap of cardboard and meat, to remove stains, to knit mufflers and wash window curtains, to smile at our husband when he came home in a bad mood, to tell him that *tanto monta monta tanto Isabel como Fernando,** that domestic economy helps to safeguard the national economy and that garlic is excellent for the bronchial tubes. We would learn to apply a bandage, to decorate a kitchen so that it looked as cute as anything, to keep our skin from chapping and cracking, and to ready with our own hands the layette for the baby destined to come into the world to be proud of the Catholic Queen, defend her from calumny, and engender children who in turn would extol her, till the end of time.

As a consequence of the brainwashing of that mawkish and optimistic propaganda of the forties, my mistrust of resolute and self-assured individuals became more marked than ever, my eagerness for freedom grew, and the alliance with disorder that I had secretly signed in the apartment on the fourth floor of No. 14 Calle Mayor turned into a near-unbreakable pact. I also put myself on my guard against the idea of getting myself a fiancé as a reward for my possible practical virtues. In those days I used to go dancing at the Casino and the back room had disappeared. But long before that, ever since the days when, as a child, I would sit myself down on the green sofa opposite this sideboard and look at the saints in the history book, neither glorious exploits nor exemplary conduct struck me as trustworthy models of behavior. Kings who stirred up wars, conquistadors and heroes disturbed me. I was suspicious of their prideful attitude as they set foot in foreign

*The famous historical motto of Ferdinand and Isabella, proclaiming their rule as coequals. *(Translator's note.)*

territory, defended forts, or planted crosses and flags. I turn toward the sideboard as though I were trying to call upon it as a witness.

How many rooms lead to this one, how many places! I would like to talk to the man in black about the narrative vehicle that is implicit in these pieces of furniture, present him with all the images that, during this interlude, have appeared to me between the sideboard and the mirror. And many more would suddenly come to mind if he were to show up here and begin to spur me on with his intermittent, off-handed questions that are not at all searching, that are like smoke rings hovering in the air. The door is ajar. I could call to him, but there's no point in it. I have no confidence in him at all. What he offers isn't confidence, on the contrary, it's something quite the opposite of confidence, something disturbing and provocative, like a continual inducement to lie. I must remember to tell him about the back room. And also about the book on romance in the postwar era. Where can that notebook possibly have gone? I'm thirsty.

The thermos is standing on the marble top of the sideboard. I pick it up and put it on a tray alongside the sugar bowl, two glasses, two spoons, and two napkins. Once I've completed this brief task, I look at the mirror, smiling. I move out of the frame, switch off the light, and the sideboard, all by itself now, fills the silver-backed surface. I walk out into the hallway, holding the tray with both hands. It is quite heavy.

REd liqht

THE FIRST THING I notice on entering the room — and it bothers me — is that the man has changed places. He is now sitting next to the table where he laid his hat down and, absorbed in contemplating something, does not raise his eyes as he hears me come into the room. I walk over to the little low table in front of the sofa, trying my best to ignore the fact that my mood has changed. It upsets me when people nose about among my things without my permission.

"Do you believe in the Devil?" I hear him ask behind my back.

My hands tremble as I set the tray down off-balance on top of the pack of cigarettes. The glasses tumble over and the sugar bowl spills. The man comes over to help me and our fingers touch.

"Your hand wasn't steady enough," he says. "Allow me."

The blood rushes to my head when I see the piece of cardboard he's carrying in his hand: my print of Luther.

"Why did you go into my bedroom?" I ask him in an annoyed tone of voice.

He bursts out laughing and that makes me even angrier.

"I don't see what's so funny," I remark.

"I'm sorry. It's just that it seemed like a phrase straight out of a serial story."

Still annoyed, I concentrate on the task of scooping up the spilled sugar with a spoon, as I mentally recite formulas to calm myself down.

"I've never entered a woman's bedroom without her consent," he says.

Once he has finished setting the glasses upright again, he takes the print back over to the big table and sets it down alongside the typewriter.

"Or perhaps," he adds, looking at the print, "you consider Luther's bedroom to be your own."

"Somebody took it out of my room!" I protest. "It's always been pinned with thumbtacks to the wall opposite my bed."

Like an imperturbable detective, the man leans over to examine the marks of the thumbtacks in the four corners of the print, then places on top of it a glass paperweight inside of which is a Gothic cathedral with iridescent columns. I walk over to where he's standing and come up behind him.

"It was right here underneath this paperweight," he assures me.

The lack of emphasis with which he says this reveals that he does not feel obliged to swear to an innocence that, for that very reason, is all the more obvious.

"But I assure you that I wasn't the one who took it out of my room," I say, deeply perturbed.

"Perhaps you don't remember. Underneath it was this handwritten verse. Is it a magic formula?"

"Let's see. . . . I have no idea."

On a sheet torn out of one of my notebooks, I see written, in my own hand, the poem that had come to my mind before, just as the storm broke:

Cabecita, cabecita,
tente en ti, no te resbales
y apareja los puntales
de la paciencia bendita.

Verás cosas
que toquen en milagrosas:
Dios delante
y San Cristóbal gigante.

"Please excuse my presumption," the man says. "But I came over here to see if it was still raining and the print and the incantation attracted my attention. I didn't think you'd mind if I looked at them."

Once I have accepted this explanation, and once he has put the papers back in the same place where he assures me that he found them, he seems to regard the subject as closed, comes back and sits down on the sofa once more, leaving me lost in thought, with my eyes fixed on the strange clues to the enigma.

"It's very odd. I don't remember when I wrote it or when I put it here."

"Is it a text you composed?"

"No, it was one that Cervantes quotes in one of his 'Exemplary Novels,' but what I don't understand . . ."

I am unable to go on. My attention has been arrested by the top of the sheet of paper peeking out above the roller of the typewriter and I am standing there paralyzed. I am so dumbfounded I am almost terrified. The phrase referring to the man on the beach has disappeared, replaced by the incantation that Cervantes's Gitanilla used to ward off heart troubles and dizzy spells. The page begins with it, copied between quotation marks, and there is nothing else written on the page, except for a number in the right-hand corner: 79. But then where are the rest of these seventy-nine pages? What are they about? The pile of papers underneath the hat seems to have grown bigger too, though I don't dare check to see.

"You still haven't told me if you believe in the Devil."

I look at the man in terror. He is unscrewing the top of the thermos bottle. He fills one of the glasses and then consults me before filling the other one.

"You wanted some too, didn't you?"

His presence is my only grip on reality at this moment, I couldn't bear it if he disappeared from my sight in a cloud of smoke. More than fear, there must be a look of entreaty in my eyes.

"What's the matter?" he asks me, holding the thermos suspended in midair.

"I'm afraid I'm about to go mad," I say, as though to myself.

"Did you say something?"

"No, nothing. Excuse me . . . but didn't you write something on my typewriter while I was in the kitchen?"

"Who, me? How absurd!"

"I don't know, I thought perhaps you might have wanted to copy the magic spell, for example. If so, I'd thank you to . . ."

"I assure you that's not the case. I haven't touched your typewriter. You want a little tea, don't you?"

"Yes, thank you."

"Well, come and get it. It's plain to see that that table is very upsetting to you."

"It's just that there are too many strange things," I say, leaning on the edge of it because I note that my legs are trembling and I'm getting light-headed.

I hold on tight to the text of the magic spell and fervently recite it to myself. The man has filled the glasses and appears to be waiting for me.

"Well," he says, "strange things happen all the time. Our mistake lies in the fact that we insist on applying the law of gravity to them, or the law of clock time, or some other law that we obey unquestioningly. It is difficult for us to admit that such things have their own law."

"Do you really believe they do?"

"Absolutely! What irritates us is that it escapes us, that we are unable to codify it. Don't you have strange dreams, for instance?"

"I certainly do. Very strange ones."

"And do you look for a logical explanation for the things you see in dreams? For the fact, for example, that one place turns into another, or one person into another?"

I shake my head. If only he'll go on talking. His words have the same hypnotic effect as those of a story. The tea shows through the glass that his hand slowly raises. All of a sudden, he seems like a magician to me. There is no telling what he may produce from underneath that hat.

"You take everything you've seen to be real, don't you? You're as certain of it as you are of your perception of this glass. . . ."

"Just as certain, yes, or perhaps even more so. And it's a sensation that stays with me for quite some time. In fact, what seems doubtful to me is what I see so clearly when I open my eyes. I miss the shadowy forms that have disappeared."

"You see? Well then, what good are those laws that appear to govern the order of time so indisputably? There's nothing that chance doesn't turn topsy-turvy."

I keep thinking, as I listen to him, of Isabel la Católica, of the deceptive version of her conduct put before us in those textbooks and those speeches, where no room was left for chance, where each step, journey, or decision of the queen appeared to bear the mark of a superior and inevitable destiny.

"If, for example, the history of Spain . . ." I start to say, without knowing where my thoughts are going to take me.

And I stop right there, in a quandary. I'd like to note down all the ideas that are rushing through my mind. I'd need some sort of thread to string them on. I must begin the book on the postwar period in a moment of sudden enlightenment like this one right now, tying together the march of history and the rhythm of dreams. It is such a vast panorama and such a topsy-turvy one, like a room where each thing is in its proper place precisely because it is out of place. All this goes back to my initial perplexities in the face of the concept of history, there in the back room, surrounded by toys and books strewn all over the floor.

"What about the history of Spain?"

"Nothing. Except that just now, when I was in the kitchen . . ."

I have spoken this last sentence in such a low voice that he must not have heard it. It vanishes, taking with it the images of my childhood and my mother's. The curtain that shuts off the door to the back room has descended again. It will go up again another time, when it chooses to do so. And as a matter of fact, he hasn't heard me. He raises the glass to his lips, takes a swallow, tastes the tea.

"It's excellent," he says. "It has exactly the right proportion of lemon, not too much and not too little."

"A relative of mine used to say that love, like lemonade, should leave you wanting just a little bit more."

He bursts out laughing. He looks younger when he laughs.

"I'll go along with that! Love that leaves you wanting just a little bit more . . . your relative wasn't mistaken on that score."

I might also use that as a starting point, the subject of love that leaves you wanting just a little bit more was a key theme of my notes: the fear of becoming sated.

"Aren't you thirsty? Or did you already drink some in the kitchen?"

"No. Why? Was I gone a long time?"

"A long time? No, it didn't seem like a long time to me. Excuse me, but do you intend to go on standing over there?"

He points to my glass and I draw closer, attracted by the liquid gleaming against the light, without being certain whether I'm walking toward him on my own two feet or being carried on the shoulders of giant Saint Christopher. I sit down next to him.

"Do you know what my answer to your question is? Yes, I believe in the Devil and in giant Saint Christopher and in blessed Barbara—in all mysterious beings, in a word. But not in Queen Isabella."

"I'm glad," he says. "You're beginning to lose your way again."

"What way do you mean?"

"The one you thought you found in the second part of *The Spa,* the way back. Do you remember the tale of Tom Thumb?"

"Yes, of course, why?"

"When he left a trail of breadcrumbs in order to find his way back, the birds ate them. He was annoyed, so the next time he left little white pebbles, and by so doing he didn't get lost, or at any rate that's what Perrault believed, that he didn't lose his way, but I'm not so sure, do you follow me?"

I smile and take a long sip of my tea.

"More or less."

"That's enough for now, we have a long night before us."

"To leave a trail of breadcrumbs?"

"That's right. The tea is good, isn't it? I'm going to help myself to some more, if you'll allow me."

I follow the movements of his slender hands above the tray. I've clearly understood now that he is in no hurry, has no particular plan in mind, and is making no effort to get to the bottom of subjects that come up. Things are merely suggested, hinted at, as in a dance whose steps we're trying out together, improvising as we go along. We have a long night before us, an open space, full of possibilities. That was exactly what that feeling of anticipation was like when I was a child having trouble dropping off to sleep. I've finally recovered, when I least expected it, that sensation of buoyancy. Only this moment exists, lie quietly, don't be distressed, all you have to do is look about the room, there's nothing you need do, little by little it will begin to be full of surprises. I take pleasure in contemplating the surfaces, the colors, the objects standing on the tray. He has now taken a tiny gold box out of his pocket. He opens it and holds it out to me. I see inside it a number of tiny pills, like pinheads, of different colors. I remain on the alert, just waiting for something to happen, feeling that I've been invited to play some unknown game. My cousins have come into the back room, bringing a parcheesi board with them. I've never seen it before. "Would you like to play?" "I don't know how." "It doesn't matter. We'll show you."

"Do you want one?"

"All right."

"Any special color?"

"Yes, mauve."

He rummages about inside, takes out a little ball, holds it up to the light and looks at it.

"It's more on the purple side," he points out. "There aren't any mauve ones. Is that all right with you?"

"Yes."

They take the counters out of a little box on the side. The top of it slides back when you put your fingernail in a groove. They are green, yellow, blue, and red. "If it's all right with you, I'll take the green ones," Peque says, and that is all right with me.

"Allow me."

I open my mouth and he places it on my tongue. I swallow it down with a little tea. It has no taste. Then he takes out a green one and swallows it.

"Just so you won't think I'm trying to poison you. You'll see how good they make you feel."

"They don't become an addiction?"

The worst part of games is that they become an addiction. That first day I was enchanted by the colored disks you could see through the glass and the strange rules of the game whereby you advanced the counters in accordance with the numbers that showed up on the die you shook in the dicebox. On the other hand, once I had learned the rules, playing parcheesi became an obligatory routine and the counters lost their bright glow. The game is now a gray cloud extending over the war years and the postwar ones, making them all alike, blurring their outlines and turning them opaque: the parcheesi years.

"An addiction? No, they're for one's memory."

"Oh? . . . They restore one's memory?"

"Well yes, they restore it, but they also disorder it, something that's very pleasant."

The tiny box with its cover now closed gleams brightly alongside the other objects on the tray. I understand that there's no point in asking whether they take effect immediately or only after some time, that the only thing that counts is to wait without knowing.

"Go on with what you were telling me," he says after a while.

"Was I telling you something?"

"Yes, when you went off to the kitchen. You were talking about lemon ice cream sandwiches."

"Oh, yes, I was. . . . They were so good."

That taste on my lips once again, Deanna Durbin once again, and skating down the highway to Zamora, and vacation time, the swifts darting back and forth like arrows at dusk above the rooftops on the square, the treasured privilege of being allowed to go out to play on the streets, of having five céntimos to buy a lemon ice cream.

"It seems to me," I say, "that I can see this very minute the place where the ice-cream vendor stood with his little cart, next to the comic book stall, in the square that our house overlooked. There was a stone bench running all the way along that side of the plaza, with an iron backrest. We used to go sit on it when we'd gotten tired of playing games. At the other end, in the first days of October, the chestnut vendor set herself up in business, with her woolen mittens. In other words, summer made its appearance on the left with the ice-cream stand, and winter announced its arrival on the right, with that smell of chestnuts that began to waft through the air from the little stall, amid whirlwinds of yellow leaves. And time passed from one end of the square to the other, imperceptibly, year after year, along that stone bench, as though slipping along a sock needle. Time passed furtively, on tiptoe. I've sometimes compared it to the rhythm of the game of Red Light, do you know it?"

"No. How is it played?"

"A child turns his back and faces a wall, leaning his arm on it and hiding his face. The others take their places behind him, at a certain distance, and come toward him, taking either small steps or running, whichever they choose. The one who's hidden his eyes says: "One, two, three, four, five . . . red light!" either quickly or slowly, as he chooses—that's the whole trick of the game, it's all up to him, and after he says that he turns around all of a sudden to see if he can catch any of the others moving. If he sees anybody moving, that person goes back to the starting line. But almost always he catches them motionless. He finds them a little closer to him, but motionless. They've come up on him without his being able to see them. We played so many games in that square—double jump rope, hopscotch, jacks, charades, ring around the rosy, run sheep run, king of the mountain. There were also games played indoors, of course, and there still are, but street games have gradually disappeared. Children play less in the streets nowadays, almost never—for one reason, no doubt, because there are so many cars now. Back then there were very few. Of the people who lived on that square, the only one who had a car was a doctor whose name was Sandoval, and it was a great event when he drove up. We got off our bicycles, and our mothers appeared on the balconies with worried looks on their faces: "Watch out, Sandoval's car is coming!" even though he drove into the square very cautiously, at less than twenty miles an hour. My father also had a car before the war, a Pontiac, but they requisitioned it."

All of a sudden, I have been transported from the Plaza de los Bandos. What a great feeling, the pill is beginning to take effect. It is nighttime and I am with my cousin Ángeles in a hotel room in Burgos. I have never slept in another city with a girlfriend. We whisper together, all excited. We are thrilled by the luxury of the room, which adjoins another with a black bathtub in it. We have the window open, who cares if there's a cold draft, it's an incomparable feeling of freedom. My father and my Uncle Vicente are staying in the room next door. They must still be talking about the business with the car. They have had long faces all during the trip and dinner, and can't keep their minds off the subject. Even when they stopped talking about it for a moment we could see by the frowns on their faces how upset they were. A few days before, papa had received an official notice informing him that his car that had gloriously served the Crusade had been wrecked and was in Burgos, but that if he came immediately and identified it, they would pay him some sort of indemnity for it. It was a late-model black Pontiac that he had bought just before the war. He asked my uncle to come with him and they decided to take us with them. It was like a dream come true. We were on our best behavior and hardly let a peep out of us during the entire trip, trying not to let our happiness show, and for that very reason when they left us alone at last it brimmed over, bordering on ecstasy. It had nothing to do with the happiness of having done our duty nor with the happiness considered appropriate to display in order to set an example of moral courage and fortitude. It was a wild happiness, inappropriate and selfish, stemming from the fact that they had left us by ourselves, that they weren't paying any attention to whether we turned the light off or not, whether we closed the window or not, that there was little chance that they'd come back to our room, because they were thinking about something else, a happiness that was ours to enjoy only because of their great distress. "I don't hear them talking. Do you suppose they've gone to sleep?" "I'm sure of it, they were very tired." "Aren't you tired?" "Who, me? Heavens no, I'm not the least bit sleepy." Through the window there came the echo of army boots, bursts of laughter, a soldier's song somewhere off in the distance:

Yo tenía un camarada,
entre todos el mejor,
siempre juntos caminábamos
siempre juntos avanzábamos,
al redoble del tambor . . .*

We leaned out the window and saw a Falangist saying goodnight to a blonde wearing lots of makeup. We saw lighted windows, open shops, street lights. An official car pulled up in front of the hotel and two men got out. The chauffeur held the door open for them. He was wearing a red beret. Later on I found out that Dionisio Ridruejo was in Burgos at that time, I read it in a book that was published last

---

*I had a comrade / the very best one of all, / we always marched together / we always advanced together / to the rolling of the drum . . . *(Translator's note.)*

year on the occasion of his death. Perhaps he was staying at that same hotel and those men were coming to see him. I suggested to my cousin that we go out for a while. At first she didn't understand, she couldn't bring herself to believe that it was possible. Then she said no, she was scared to. "Oh, come on, girl, why not? They won't even know we're gone." I convinced her. We silently primped in front of the bathroom mirror; the washbasin was also black. We walked out into the hall, there wasn't a sign of light coming from underneath their door. We went down the carpeted stairway on tiptoe without meeting a soul, scarcely daring to breathe. We left the room key with the desk clerk. In the dining room there were unknown people, it may be that I met some of them later on, it may be that Dionisio Ridruejo was in there. "Do you think the desk clerk will say anything to our fathers tomorrow?" "Of course not, don't be silly, he didn't even look at us." We'd painted our lips slightly, so as to look older, with a stick of red cocoa butter that Ángeles had. Very few people noticed us but it seemed as though everybody was staring at us. We walked only a short way, just down to the Espolón, the lights were gleaming on the river. Walking was like flying. "I for one am going to stay up all night, I can tell you that right now." And all of a sudden she got scared, she said they might lock the hotel doors and that would be awful. We walked back. It seemed to her that the street wasn't the same one we'd taken before, that we were going to get lost, but I was able to orient myself perfectly. Unfortunately we were very close already, and I had not neglected to leave little white pebbles behind: "There it is right over there, can't you see it?" "*You* ask for the key." "All right, but don't look at the desk clerk, okay? Just go right in as though it were the most natural thing in the world." The hotel had a revolving door and I went through it first. There was a young married couple standing at the desk. "The key to room 307 please." My voice came out sounding like a dubbed film. The clerk gave the key to us, we went upstairs in the elevator with the couple: "What floor do you want to get off at?" "The fourth." They were going up to the sixth. "Good night." And once again the two of us were alone in our room, with the door closed. We found it hysterically funny that that couple had addressed us using the formal *ustedes,* as though we were grown-ups, and it fascinated us to think that maybe they were newlyweds. We put the beds together so as to go on talking in low voices. We heard a clock strike two. Laughter and sleeplessness circulated inside us like tickling sensations, while outside we were surrounded by that city that might have been Manhattan or Los Angeles or wherever it was that Deanna Durbin was sleeping at that moment, smiling, stuffed full of ice cream, pleasantly fatigued after so much skating.

The following morning we went downstairs to have breakfast, with uneasy consciences and mingled feelings of complicity and anxiety. Nothing. The desk clerk hadn't said a word to them. They still had long faces, but for the same reason as the day before, on account of the car. All they could talk about was going to recover the remains of the car, as though they were about to attend a ceremony that was something like a funeral. The four of us left the hotel, it was early and there was a bit of fog, and on the streets were garbage trucks, priests, ladies in mantillas on their way to mass, office clerks. The city had lost all its strangeness. The automobile graveyard was on the outskirts of town. It was a sort of very large shed, with a huge pile of skeletons of vehicles that were charred, riddled with holes, or split in half, lying any which way, in whatever position they had fallen, as in a garbage dump. We stopped in front of that mountain of rust, the two of us lagging behind a little and as I put my arm around my cousin's shoulder, I thought — I remember it very well — that those cars had once been new. In order to see them as they were when they were new I had only to call upon my imagination, remember the look of displeasure that had come across my parents' faces on being confronted with a puncture, a few flaking flecks of paint on the fenders, or a pothole in the pavement which, if it had been raining, might have caused mud to spatter on the gleaming bodywork. "It's a black Pontiac," my father said to the man in charge. It took them a long time to find it, because everything was all mixed up there, because the war had mixed up everything. The two of us followed the others at a certain distance, threading our way, with the sort of religious fear that keeps one from treading on grave markers, through the heaps of scrap iron, the tires, and the disemboweled seats strewn all over that junk shed. My father and my uncle preceded us, accompanied by the man in charge of this graveyard, a pug-nosed individual dressed in blue coveralls who, on our arrival, once certain papers had been exchanged, had fallen into step with them, whistling the while. In the very gesture whereby my father had removed from his wallet that paper that he handed over to the man, I had realized that he was going about things in his typical professional manner and naturally that reassured me, making me wonder, at some point in our peregrinations, whether the whole thing might not be a dream, at the end of which the Pontiac would reappear, all in one piece and undamaged. That, of course, would have been a happy ending absolutely in accord with the way things always turned out in romantic novels. But then, at a certain moment all of us stopped, because the man in coveralls, after inspecting a heap of twisted metal and consulting his paper, had left off whistling and halted in his tracks. "There's your car," he said to my father, "and surely they'll be able to give you up to a thousand pesetas, because the engine's still good and can be salvaged," and he raised the rusted remains of the hood. The mere mention of this figure, which struck me as being a great deal of money, helped me to escape from that junkheap to the city that I had caught a glimpse of the night before. I wandered through it, dizzied and beside myself with excitement, without my cousin this time, since all she would have done was raise objections, all by myself with a thousand pesetas in my purse, as though I had stolen that sum. "They must think we're stealing money," my father used to say, as the supreme insult, when prices went up. "I don't know how people live these days, where do they get the money?" I had gotten it from a robbery, I had given my cousin the slip, I was wandering about loose in the city, I was a very wicked girl. It was an extremely brief escape. My eyes immediately met my father's and that recourse to dreams turned into a shameful sin. He stood there motionless in front of the corpse of the late-model black Pontiac, very nearly in tears, and Uncle Vicente had put a hand on his shoulder. But what lent the scene the greatest weight of reality was the presence of the man in the blue coveralls. His indifference, which he concealed only with the greatest of difficulty, destroyed the harmony of the tableau and totally excluded him from what was going on, but on the other hand, the fact that he formed such a visible part of it was what kept one from entertaining the hope that all that was not really happening. "Well, it's up to you, if you'll come to the office with me and give me a signature as verification of the fact that you've identified it, because it is your car, right?" He was proving to be the most tangible, the most inescapable thing in the world, with his pug nose and his little bowlegs. "Come on, man, don't take it so hard," Uncle Vicente said. "We've at least saved our skins. Just remember poor Joaquín." I looked at him. A few months previously he had arrived at our house one morning, hugged my mother, and then the two of them had sat down on the bench in the hall for a long time, shedding tears for the death of their older brother. It was a bench with a seat that could be raised, and was used for storing magazines. In issues of one of them, called *Cronica,* dating back to the time of the Republic, were photographs of female nudes taken by a man named Manassé, Uncle Joaquín used to make risqué remarks about them that were not fit for children's ears. He was tall and handsome and a bit brazen. They accused him of being a Socialist and shot him to death. Whenever he came to see us, he brought us presents. He was the one who gave us the parcheesi set. But that was before.

"And why is it that you've compared the passage of time with the game of Red Light?" the man in black asks me.

I look at him. He is holding the glass of tea in his hand and contemplating the transparent liquid as though he were looking in a mirror. The Burgos hotel episode was nice, I'd forgotten all about it for a long time now.

"Because that's more or less how it is, time steals by so furtively that we don't even notice, we don't see it passing. But all of a sudden we turn around and find images that have moved behind our backs, frozen photographs that bear no dates, like the figures of the children in the game of Red Light, who could never be caught moving. That's why it's so difficult later on to put the things we remember in order, to be sure of what happened before and what happened later."

I interrupt myself. The Burgos hotel episode must have been in '38. I ought to note it down, otherwise I'll forget. I glance over toward the table, feeling the urge to rise to my feet and get a sheet of paper, and I have the impression that the pile underneath the hat has increased in size. I look away. I'd be better off writing it down in a notebook. I keep losing loose sheets of paper.

"Knowing for sure what came before and what came after! We're back to the subject of little white pebbles again. The disorder in which memories come to mind is their only guarantee, little white pebbles aren't to be trusted. Were you looking for something?"

I have risen to my feet as he is speaking, and have begun rummaging about in the drawer of a piece of furniture with a mirror that is standing to his right, blocking off the sofa on that side. It seems to me that I must have put the notebook with my jottings about the postwar period in it, though naturally what would be more amusing at the moment would be to find copies of *Crónica,* that magazine with the female nudes photographed by Manassé.

"Yes, a notebook that must be somewhere around here. I never remember where I put things. . . ." I pull out magazines, photographs taken at different periods, a deck of cards, receipts, file folders, dumping everything on the floor with brusque gestures.

"Do you need it for something right now?"

"Yes, to note down the Burgos episode. The thing is, in talking with you so many things are beginning to come to light . . . and they're all mixed up."

The rubber bands around a beige folder that I've just grabbed out of the drawer give way, it spills open, and a whole bunch of newspaper clippings scatter all over the floor. I kneel down to pick them up, and the man in turn makes a move to bend over.

"May I help you?"

"No thanks, don't bother."

There is a label pasted on the cover of the folder, on which I've written in capital letters: FANTÔMES DU PASSÉ. Among the clippings I see a photo of Conchita Piquer, and I stop to have a closer look at it. She is raising a glass of manzanilla to her parted lips and is looking at me out of the corner of her proud, bitter eyes. The same thing happens whenever I open a drawer. Something different from what I was hunting for turns up, something that I had been searching for days ago. This time it's an article of mine, published in *Triunfo,* one on postwar songs. It may help give me ideas for the book when I get seriously to work on it.

"What was the Burgos episode?" the man asks. I look up at him from the floor.

"I beg your pardon? The Burgos hotel episode you mean? . . . Nothing, really, just that time when we went to get the car that they'd requisitioned from my father. I told you about it just a while ago, didn't I?"

He shrugs and purses his lips as a sign that he doesn't understand. Then he shakes his head slowly from right to left.

"What do you mean I didn't tell you?"

I sit down alongside the papers strewn all over the floor, with a sudden feeling of isolation. There is a silence.

"Don't bite your fingernails like that," the man says. "What happened in Burgos? You have strange ways of running away."

"What happens to me since I've become hard of hearing is horrible," I say in a dull voice. "I can't tell the difference between what I say aloud and what I think to myself. I'm going to have to go see the doctor."

"But I don't understand. What does your hearing have to do with it? I grant that deafness might have an effect on what you say, but not on what you don't say."

"It's not that simple, it's also a feeling of inner vertigo that makes everything even more confused. Since my hearing's gotten worse, I've lost my sense of security. It's as though I'm groping my way along."

I look once more at the photo of Conchita in her heyday.

Quien va por el mundo a tientas
*lleva los rumbos perdíos . . .**

she used to sing.

It seems as though her parted lips are about to move to sing the second part of the song. Her songs always had a second part, usually an unhappy ending. Heart on the alert, her listener prepared to shed tears. I remember her standing, hieratic and expectant, staring into space, filling that solemn pause with just her presence, making it a sort of entr'acte that she was creating between the opening verses and the end of those stories of love and heartbreak.

No sé qué mano cristiana
cortó una mañana
mi venda de repente . . .†

was one of her most touching songs, about a woman who has been deceived by her lover, but doesn't want to admit it to herself, a theme very characteristic of those years, when resignation, fatalism, and pretense prevailed. The title of it was "Blindly," or perhaps "Groping My Way Along." You don't hear that song on the new records that come out these days.

"Anyone who gropes his way through this world has lost his bearings," I say, absorbed in my own thoughts. But this time my voice is audible and the man has caught my words.

---

*Anyone who gropes his way through this world / has lost his bearings . . .

†I don't know what charitable hand / suddenly cut away / my blindfold one morning . . . *(Translator's note.)*

"Well, don't let it prey on your mind like that, it's not that serious a problem if one loses one's bearings."

I could explain that they're words from one of Piquer's songs, or simply stand up, throw a black shawl over my shoulders, and without further introduction lean my back against the wall and sing him the song, which is now coming back to my mind, my throat, my tear ducts, word for word, but I merely shrug and twist my body around slightly, thus leaving my back resting against the bottom edge of the sofa, alongside his outstretched legs. It has stopped raining, but there is a strong wind blowing.

"What's the trouble? Aren't you going to go on looking for the notebook?"

"No, it doesn't matter," I say in a long-suffering tone of voice.

Through the French door, I see the silhouette of a towel hanging on the clothesline, whipping back and forth in the wind and flapping against the terrace railing. It must be soaking wet, like all the laundry that I hung out to dry in the afternoon, but it doesn't matter, nothing matters. I am far away, on an island. The word *isolation* comes from the word *island*. It was a dangerous feeling, forbidden by the instructresses in the Women's Section. When a person deliberately fosters it, it leads to a martyr complex. There is something sick and irrational in that vague pleasure at feeling misunderstood, a feeling that has no real basis in fact and is not directed against anyone in particular, that causes the individual to wallow in enjoyable self-pity. To indulge in it is to withdraw into a fortified castle, to turn the literary image of raising all one's drawbridges into something grand and glorious.

"Come, come, my dear, don't get upset. Just tell me about that hotel in Burgos business, and that will be the end of it."

"Never mind, it's of no importance. It was a memory of the war years, but it's vanished now."

I see one of the stranger's hands appear before my eyes, holding out a ballpoint pen and a little memo book to me. I wasn't expecting such a thing and am a bit startled.

"What's this?"

"Nothing. They're for you to use in case you want to write something down about the Burgos episode. Didn't you want to make a note about it?"

"Oh, yes, thank you. Although as a matter of fact it no longer . . ."

I take the objects he's holding out to me. What I took for a ballpoint pen turns out to be an old-fashioned green mechanical pencil. I look at it in bewilderment. It has no visible point, one has to turn a little gold wheel at the lower end of the pencil to make it appear. On noting how clumsily I am going about it, the man shows me how, without a word, limiting himself to guiding my fingers with the tips of his from behind me, leaning down toward me just long enough to do so and not a moment more, whereupon he must have assumed his original position, since his legs, which I can see in front of me, are now stretched out again. I raise my knees up, place the memo book on them and sit there looking out at the soaking wet towel, not knowing what to write down. But on the other hand, not putting anything down would be impolite. Finally I note down, reluctantly, in big handwriting: "Automobile graveyard. Burgos. 1938?" I slowly tear out the page marked off in little squares and lay it down on the floor, on top of the newspaper clippings scattered all about, fully aware of the futility of my gesture and of the uncertain future that awaits this bit of paper lost in the midst of so many other bits of paper.

"It's the way it is with dreams," I say. "It's always exactly the same."

"Exactly the same in what way?"

"There's always the same eagerness to note down things that seem to be urgent, the same scribbling of disconnected words on loose scraps of paper, in notebooks, and all for what? As soon as I see my handwriting, the things it refers to turn into dried-up butterflies that just a while before were flitting about in the sunlight. That's exactly what happens to me when I wake up from a dream: I seize on what I've just seen as though it were a fundamental message. Nobody could possibly convince me, at that moment, that any more important key for understanding the world exists than the one that the dream, however nonsensical it may have been, has just suggested to me, but the minute I start looking around for a pencil it's gone. Nothing coincides or holds together, the thread that the beads of the necklace were strung on has broken. Nonetheless, I never learn, I'm confronted on every hand with the trace of those futile efforts. I live surrounded by scraps of paper on which I've tried in vain to chase down phantoms and record important messages, and I hang on to the pencil out of sheer inertia, do you understand what I mean? I know it's a stupid vice, but it calms my nerves."

The man sitting at my back doesn't say a word. There's no telling if he's even still there. I turn toward him and give him back the green mechanical pencil and the memo book with little pages ruled off in squares.

"Thank you. And please excuse me."

He puts them in the pocket of his jacket.

"What is it I'm supposed to excuse you for?"

"Running away."

Perhaps the proper thing to do now would be to kneel at his feet and bow my head, waiting for my penance. Running away always met with severe punishment.

"I like it very much when you run away," he says, with a disconcertingly gentle smile. "As far as I'm concerned you can run away as much as you like. You do it very well."

I search for some pretext to lessen the intensity of the silence that ensues, and I find it when my eyes light on the gleaming little gold box lying on the tray. I lean forward, trying to make my gesture of pointing toward it with my chin seem natural, as I reach for my half-empty glass of tea.

"It's no doubt the effect of those pills," I say.

And because I've meant my tone of voice to be bantering, it sounds forced to me, like repartee in a bad comedy. These flashes of self-criticism never leave any room for doubt. My conclusions always prove to be perfectly correct. The man's immediate reply confirms my impression.

"Don't keep defending yourself all the time. We agreed that there was no point in it. You're a born escapist, and what's more you know you are, so kindly don't use those pills as a shield to hide behind now."

I ought to turn around and look him straight in the face, but I feel that I can't, that I'd be sure to blush.

"Me an escapist? That's really funny, nobody's ever told me a thing like that before."

"Are you certain of that?"

I don't know what to do with my glass. It's in my way there in my hand, but in cases such as this, it's better not to move, better just to go along with the situation.

"I don't believe so."

"Nobody may have told you so, but it's obvious. And besides, there's nothing wrong in that. The only bad thing, that is to say bad for you, is that you try to justify yourself."

I put the glass down on the floor, hug my knees, and sit there without a word, lost in thought, beneath the spell of his strange absolution. He has told me that I'm an escapist, he has told me so without the slightest reproach. Why, if this pleases me, should it also upset me? The fear comes to me from a long way back, from the years of the back room, from newspapers, from pulpits and confessionals, from the indignant whispers of ladies watching me pass by in the street, from behind their raised curtains, as I head down to the river with boys who are friends of mine. None of them is my intended, nor even my sweetheart, but they sing and laugh and hold my hand. We walk down narrow back streets, we drop into taverns, we rent a boat to go rowing on the Río Tormes, which has just thawed. There's an early spring sun shining. "She's turned out to be a brazen little hussy." "She does whatever she jolly well pleases." No, that doesn't have anything to do with me, that was before, I'm getting the war and the postwar years all mixed up. That was what they said of the girls who used to go out by themselves for a stroll with Italian soldiers on the

Campo de Francisco as it was getting dark and come home late for dinner, with flaming cheeks and a new necklace. Everything went to pieces during the war, it destroyed all standards of decency and integrity. There were big profits to be made fishing in those troubled waters. People no longer came by money honestly: "There's dirty business afoot." "There's something shady going on there." All people wanted was to save their skins, to have a good time, to survive. It was a madness that spread to women too. Money, money, where can they be getting the money from? These were syncopated comments I kept hearing without understanding them at all and pondered in the back room. "That one—where can she be getting the money from? She's a bold one, she is." It seemed horrifying to me that somebody might possibly say of me some time that I was a bold one. Today boldness is a synonym for spontaneity, something a woman flaunts to prove her lack of preconceived ideas and inhibitions. A woman who's repressed today is the object of a sarcasm that is the precise equivalent of yesterday's condemnation of the bold woman. Boldness was a tempting and ambiguous attribute of freedom, as was madness, its close kin.

"That one? She's a madwoman." And a strict law punishing any attempted prison break applied to all those anomalous and defiant patterns of behavior. Madwomen, bold women, scatterbrained women were skirting the limits of transgression, and the order to halt in their tracks inevitably rang out the moment they made their getaway. "The alarm has sounded. She's escaped." There were no extenuating circumstances, the condemnation was total, it was a blot on the family honor that could scarcely be mentioned, a disgrace proclaimed by mute gesticulations, as in scenes in silent films. We children were obliged to figure out the details of that ominous text from the gestures, but the general outlines were laid down in accordance with a dichotomy that was only too comprehensible: staying put, conforming, and making the best of things was good; skipping out, escaping, running away were bad. Yet at the same time they were the heroic thing to do, since Don Quixote, Christ, and Saint Teresa had fled, had abandoned home and family. That was where the contradiction lay, and the answer they gave us was that all of them had done so in the name of a lofty ideal and that theirs was a noble madness. The child's timid questions inevitably were dashed to pieces against those vague terms "lofty ideal" and "noble madness," thus whetting his or her curiosity and turning it into a secret anxiety. I thought it might also be heroic to escape simply because one felt like it, out of love of freedom and of happiness — not that official, circumspect happiness imposed by fiat, but rather that hearty laughter and that song that come pouring forth from a spring whose waters no one channels — a thought I kept entirely to myself and one that involved furtively giving in to the temptation of imagining how the voices, the faces, and the bodies of those bold lovers who had provoked, by their escape, the unanimous condemnation of all of society would be transformed once they were beyond the sight of others' eyes. I imagined them in my dreams and admired their courage, though I would not have dared confess this to anyone. Just as I would never have dared flee from the light of the sun, I knew that I would escape, rather, by way of the dark, secret twists and turns of imagination, by way of the spiral of dreams, by way of a path within, without creating a scandal or breaking down walls. I knew that everyone was born to follow his own path.

I look at the wall opposite. "The World Turned Topsy-Turvy": my eyes find sanctuary in the cheap print marked off in yellow rectangles. The figures that appear in them are celebrating a sacred ritual. I am there too, I too have a role to play in acting out that story. Escaping without venturing outside, more difficult still, a mad undertaking, contrary to the laws of gravity and the tangible, the world turned topsy-turvy for certain. But even more topsy-turvy than the lamb with a hat and the sun fallen to earth and the fish flying through the air that I see depicted there in front of me, even more absurd than that is what they might be seeing, if they had eyes to see: the judge has discovered the fugitive, has absolved him and admonished him to continue to escape whenever he wishes. It's enough to make a person burst into sidesplitting laughter, the absurdity of what's happening to me makes me a rival of all those saints of the absurd.

The man leans over toward me and takes hold of one of my elbows.

"I beg your pardon, but wouldn't you be more comfortable sitting here beside me? Or are you going to go on searching for that notebook?"

"What notebook? . . . Ah . . . no, no."

"Well then, don't run away all by yourself. I like it better when you do so aloud."

I allow him to help me to my feet. I sit down next to him, smile at him.

"Or at least if you run away all by yourself, tell me afterwards what you've seen. Where did you go wandering off to just now? Back to Burgos again?"

"No, I took a boat ride on the Tormes."

"By yourself?"

"No, with some friends from my first-year class at the university."

"Was it an enjoyable boat ride?"

"It was a little cold. The river had just thawed, though I'm not really certain of that. I think I may be wrong. The worst cold spells were during the war. I could swear that in the forties the Tormes didn't freeze over. I'll have to ask my sister, she'll remember. It was a short boat ride, it seems to me that some ladies who were watching me from their balcony made nasty remarks about me too, but I'm not sure, maybe the remarks weren't about me. Several different images came to my mind at the same time. My memories of the war and the postwar years are always all mixed up. That's why I'm finding it difficult to write the book."

"What book?"

"Haven't I told you about it already?"

"No, but don't start worrying about that now. Perhaps you told me and I didn't hear you. Please tell me again, if you'll be so kind."

"It's a book I have in mind about mores and affairs of the heart in those days."

"The days of the lemon ice cream?"

"Yes, and of parcheesi, and of Carmencita Franco. The idea for the book came to me in fact on the very morning of her father's funeral, when I saw her on television."

"And what's become of that project?"

"I lost all enthusiasm for it. It was other people's reminiscences that killed it. You may have noticed how many memoirs have come out since Franco's death. They're a real epidemic now, and in the final analysis that's what discouraged me, the thought that, if other people's memoirs bore me, why wouldn't mine bore other people?"

"Don't write it in the form of a book of memoirs then."

"Ah, that's where the whole trouble lies. I'm waiting to see whether I can hit on some entertaining way of stringing my memories together."

"Or of unstringing them."

"Or of unstringing them — yes of course, there's that too. You'll have to leave me that little box of pills."

"It's yours. I was planning on leaving it with you."

"Oh, please, I only meant that as a joke."

"Maybe *you* did, but *I* didn't. Ever since I left home, it was my intention to give it to you."

"Really? Why is that?"

"Just because, that's all. For you to keep as a sort of amulet."

It lies gleaming on the tray, I pick it up and begin to fondle it, turning it over and over in my fingers.

"Thank you. I really will write the book now."

The moment I say this, the thought occurs to me that I promised that very same thing to Todorov in January. Back then, of course, what I was going to write was a fantastic novel. I've just had an idea. What if I combined the two promises into one?

"Talk to me about the book, would you like to?"

"It's not that I wouldn't like to, it's just that I don't know where to begin, I'm having so much difficulty with that book . . . or rather, it isn't a book yet. What else would you like . . ."

"If it were already a book we wouldn't be having such an entertaining night. It's only when we're in the process of doing things that they're worthwhile, don't you think?"

"That's true, as soon as we finish one thing, we have to invent something else."

"Well then, it's better if it's taking a long time . . . let's see, tell me how the idea of writing the book came to you."

"We're going to get way off the track."

"The track of what?"

"Of what the book is about."

"What does that matter? We'll end up somewhere in any case; and when you come right down to it, as far as getting lost is concerned, we've already been lost for quite some time. Or maybe you haven't?"

"Oh, yes, I certainly have been."

"And besides, telling how the idea of writing it came to you is already like beginning to write it, even though you never do, so what does it matter?"

"You're right. The thing is that I'd have to do a good job of telling you about it, otherwise it isn't worth the trouble."

"And who's asking you to tell me about it badly? You're not in any hurry, I presume."

"No, I'm not. How about you?"

"I'm in no hurry either. So go ahead with your story. It's the morning of Franco's funeral, is that right?"

He has sprawled out on the sofa and is looking toward the terrace, with an air of concentration and pleasure, as though he had guessed that the best part of the story is about to begin. For a fleeting moment I miss, once again, not having a fireplace here in the corner, with its red and blue flames; good stories are always forthcoming (at least in our imagination) in the warm glow of a fire on the hearth.

"Well, in order for you to understand what I felt that morning, I have to go back quite a way, to Salamanca again."

"Go back as far as you need to."

"Before Franco, my notions of what might be happening in the country were very vague; I was born right in the middle of Primo de Rivera's dictatorship, on December 8, 1925, the same day that Pablo Iglesias and Antonio Maura died . . . but never mind, that's a coincidence that doesn't mean anything."

"How do you know? It may very well mean something."

"I don't know. Anyway, what I'm trying to say is that up until I was nine years old, politics seemed to me to be a complicated and incomprehensible puzzle, something far away that I needn't bother my head about, a game for the amusement of big people. But I noticed that they had fun playing that game. They quite naturally fell into heated discussions about its ins and outs, in loud voices, and it didn't appear to be a monotonous game, but rather one with lots of variety. Colored cards with new figures kept appearing all the time, and each player announced his preference for this one or that, just as we children might like Shirley Temple better than Laurel and Hardy, find *Jeromín* a better comic book than *T.B.O.,* or parcheesi a better game than snakes and ladders. I remember that once, after the Republic was proclaimed, my Uncle Joaquín, who had joined the Socialist party, came back from Madrid with a very funny tongue twister that he had learned there, a sort of rebus for initiates that, as I found out later on studying the history of that period, had to do with certain shady dealings that had caused Lerroux and other politicians to lose their reputations, recounted in terms of a game of chance called *estraperlo* that had recently been imported from abroad and was sweeping the country. My parents laughed uproariously at this conundrum, and since I was very quick at committing poetry and the words of songs to memory, I immediately learned it by heart and recited it, to the delight of everyone. It went: 'El estraperlo es una especie de ruleta que tiene dos colores: *le blanc* y *le rouge.* Si tires al azar, sale una bolita que hace "pich y pon." Si no aciertas tu número s'han perdido los dineros. Si aciertas dices: Venzo, y puedes irte, galante, a comer de baldivia, y nadie podrá decir: ése derrocha el dinero.'"*

"What made it funny, of course, was that the names of Leblanc, Lerroux, Salazar, Pich y Pon, Samper, Benzo,

*Literally: "*Estraperlo* is a sort of roulette that has two colors: *le blanc* and *le rouge.* If you try your luck, a little ball comes out that goes 'pich and pon.' If you haven't bet on the right number, you've lost all your money. If you have, you say: I win, and you can go off, you gay blade, to eat dinner for free, and nobody can say to you: that guy's squandering his money." *(Translator's note.)*

Galante, Valdivia, and Rocha appeared, slightly camouflaged, in the text. My uncle explained to me, for he was never one to leave a child's curiosity unsatisfied: 'They're politicians in Madrid, do you understand?' And I was more convinced than ever that politics was a game of chance combinations, like solitaire, a harmless guessing game. After the war, however, the word *estraperlo* no longer had any connection in people's minds with roulette, for it had come to mean the black market. It had become something sordid and depressing. Those secretly permitted under-the-counter dealings in contraband goods that raised the price of everything and made it hard to get rice, oil, coal, and potatoes were no laughing matter. It was a name that made people's faces turn sad when they uttered it and it is forever associated in my mind with other oft-repeated expressions of the time that have the same color of ashes: Tax Fraud Tribunal, ration card, Supply and Transportation Office — institutions related to the need to survive, to punishment and scarcity, a hotbed of paperwork and problems that couldn't possibly amuse anyone. . . . But I'm wandering all over hill and dale, do please excuse me."

An absent smile flits across the man's lips, and he looks at me with a certain impatience.

"Stay up in the hills; you're far too inclined to stick to the easy paths down in the dales."

"What I wanted to tell you was that before the war, when I heard talk of Azaña, of Gil Robles, of Lerroux, or of King Alfonso XIII, who was in exile, or when I saw their pictures in the papers, they seemed to me to be as unreal as Wifredo the Hairy or the jack of clubs, figures in a deck of cards that you could use to make all sorts of combinations, as you chose. I couldn't believe that they really existed or that they ruled anybody's life, and I found it even more impossible to imagine that they might have something to do with me or might keep me from doing something, whether it was eating chocolate or telling my playmates who lived on the same street that I had an uncle who was a Socialist. People talked about whatever they liked, played whatever game they liked, and that was all there was to it as far as I could see. So from that point of view Franco was the first real ruler in my life that I was ever aware of as such, because from the beginning it was clear that he was the one and only, that his power was indisputable and omnipresent, that he had managed to insinuate himself into all the houses, schools, movie theaters, and cafés, do away with spontaneity and variety, arouse a religious, uniform fear, stifle conversations and laughter so that no one's voice rang out any louder than anyone else's. You must remember that I was nine years old when I began to see his picture everywhere, in the newspapers and on the walls, smiling beneath that military beret with the tassel, and then later on in the classrooms of the Institute and in the newsreels at the movies and on stamps. And the years went by and there was always his effigy and nothing but his effigy. The others were satellites, his reign was absolute. If he was ill nobody knew it, it seemed as though sickness and death could never touch him. So that when he died, my reaction was the same as that of many other people, I couldn't believe it. There were those who loudly rejoiced and celebrated. There may have been others who wept, I wouldn't deny that, but I was as unmoved as a rock.

All the years of his reign came tumbling down on top of me. To me they felt like a homogeneous block, like a dark red-brown mountain range such as the ones shown on geophysical maps. The one thing I realized, as I told you before, was that I am simply not capable of discerning the passage of time all during that period, or differentiating the war years from the postwar ones. The thought came to me that Franco had paralyzed time, and on the very day that they were about to bury him I woke up, with my mind focused on that one thought with a very special intensity. And I remembered that they had said that they were going to televise the funeral. I don't have a television set and hardly ever watch anything on TV, but that day I made an exception and went with my daughter and a girlfriend of hers to a bar downstairs. It's a crowded, noisy bar catering to people who happen to be passing by. It has a permanent smell of fried squid and, it goes without saying, a television set.

"Yes," the man says. "And the worst of it is that it's right above the phone and nobody can hear anything. That's where I called you from before."

I am surprised that he says "before," and not last month or last year. I'm finding it hard to calculate how long he's been sitting here.

"Yes, of course, that's the place, the Peru Bar. It was full of people, and I noticed, as I was watching the images of the funeral procession making its way toward the Valley of the Fallen, that the noise of all the conversations kept getting louder and louder and more and more people kept pouring in. There were faces of people from the neighborhood that I recognized—the fruit-seller downstairs, a woman who sells lottery tickets, several doormen from buildings along the street, doctors from the Social Security Clinic. A discussion began between the bartender and several customers over the bar counter as to whether or not it was sheer insanity that thousands of people who lived in Madrid had spent three days and nights in a row waiting in line to catch a brief glimpse of the body when it was exposed to public view: 'They did that because if people don't see a thing like that they don't believe it,' somebody said, and other people spontaneously expressed their views on the subject, perhaps because they felt that everyone had a right to his own opinion with regard to this funeral. Many of them held the view that that was the least that could be done for a person who had ruled the destiny of the country for such a long time. Others contested that opinion, but it was a free and dispassionate discussion, it seemed as though the words 'ruled,' 'destiny,' and 'country' had been stripped of their official uniform and were lying stark naked on a dissection table so that the autopsy could be performed. There were also remarks, naturally, to the effect that it had taken Franco a long time to die. Some people commented on the fact with a hint of pity in their voices, but the comments of most of them were tinged with macabre, barefaced humor, aimed especially at the baroque terminology of the communiqués that had been issued to describe the illness that in the end had sent Franco, however much he might have appeared to be the sempiternal *caudillo,* to the massive tomb that awaited him, with the gravestone appearing there on the television screen alongside the yawning empty hole into which he would be lowered. But the oppressive and well-nigh abject progress of that illness, that was mindful of a biblical curse and that had kept us glued to the radio for weeks and weeks, was now tending to retreat into the background of the comments that people were making, because Madrilenians adapt themselves to the present unusually quickly. . . . But I must surely be boring you with all these digressions."

"No, you bore me only when you stop."

"I'm just going to have a little tea."

I put the little gold box that I've been fondling all this time back down on the tray, lean over to pick up the glass of tea from the floor, and drain it in one swallow. It has left a circle on the photograph of Conchita Piquer, right on top of her glass of manzanilla. I now set my glass down empty on the table. The man attentively observes each of these gestures punctuating this respite.

"Well then, we've come to the business about the book now. You'll remember that it was on the twenty-third of November that Franco was buried."

"Yes, I remember, but what does that have to do with the book?"

"Wait, you'll see, it does have a connection, sometimes the little white pebbles not only serve to mark the path, but to lead us backwards. They can combine in a magical way. There I was, watching the television set, my mind in a daze from the noise in the bar, but nothing had yet happened to take me away from that spot, properly speaking, until the announcer suddenly said: '. . . on this sunny morning of November 23,' and then and there, with the mention of that date, everything began to be transformed, because of it I fled backward, to the origins."

"What origins?"

"My own. I realized that in just two weeks it would be my fiftieth birthday, because I too was born at noon, and on a morning with lots of sun. My mother has told me so. Moreover, it had something of a historical flight about it at the same time. It was a double flight backward. I remembered that the deaths of Antonio Maura and Pablo Iglesias had coincided with my birth, and it suddenly came to me that a cycle of fifty years was about to end, that my entire life had unfolded between those two funerals that I had not seen and the one that I was seeing. I felt as though I were framed by that circle revolving about me, with two sunny mornings as poles. And as I was thinking this and beginning to look at the television set in another way, as though it were a crystal ball from which omens and unexpected signs can be conjured up, I saw that the funeral delegation was arriving at the Valley of the Fallen and that Carmencita Franco had just appeared on the screen. That image served as the basic catalyst: seeing her walking along slowly, dressed in mourning and with that bitter, empty expression that her face has been set in for years now, hidden only with the greatest of difficulty by her official smile, brought back to my mind with total clarity that other morning that I saw her in Salamanca with her crocheted socks and her little black patent leather slippers, coming out of the cathedral. 'No one recognizes her,' I thought, 'but she's that same girl. She wouldn't recognize me either. We've grown up and lived in the same years. She was the daughter of an army officer from the provinces. We've been the victims of the same manners and mores, we've read the same magazines and seen the same movies. Our children may be different, but our dreams have surely been much the same, I'm as certain of that as I am of all the other things that can never be proved.' And I was touched to see her walk on toward the hole in the ground in which they were going to put that man, who for her was simply her father, whereas for all other Spaniards he had been the devious and secret motive force of that block of time, the chief engineer and the inspector and the manufacturer of the transmission gears, and time itself, whose flow he had damped, damned, and directed, with the result that one barely felt either time or him move, and the imperceptible variations that inevitably came about, merely because of the passage of time, in language, in dress, in music, in human relations, in public entertainment, in places, seemed to have simply fallen from heaven. And naturally I had escaped completely from the place we were in at that moment, and from my daughter and my daughter's girlfriend, who were having a beer at the counter. I saw them there in their blue jeans and it seemed impossible to me to explain to them my sudden emotion at the sight of Carmencita Franco, bereaved of that sempiternal father, who sometimes was photographed with her by the press in inaccessible rooms, during brief respites from his dictatorial vigilance. It was all over, never again. Time unfroze. The man responsible for checking its flow and presiding over it had disappeared. Franco officially opening factories and reservoirs, decreeing death penalties, giving his daughter and the daughters of his daughter in marriage, speaking over the radio, watching the annual parade commemorating Victory, Franco fishing for trout, Franco in the Pazo de Meirás, Franco on postage stamps, Franco in the newsreels, as we all grew older with him, under him. The funeral procession entered the Basilica and we again saw the open grave. 'They're going to bury him,' I thought, but it was a thought quite far removed from any political considerations. I was asking myself, rather, what this block of time had been like. I was thinking of it from the point of view of the game of Red Light. I don't know if you follow me or not."

"Yes, of course I do."

"It was then that I realized I knew all about that period. I went upstairs to my apartment, and began to jot things down in a notebook. That's the notebook I was looking for a while ago."

I glance over toward the piece of furniture with the mirror. The drawer is still open and there are still things inside it, the notebook surely must be in there.

"That's a marvelous story," the man says. "And what happened then? Did you lose your enthusiasm for the whole project?"

"Yes, but I don't remember when. In the beginning, I spent several months going to the periodicals library to consult newspapers and magazines, and then I realized that that wasn't how to go about it, that what I was trying to recapture was something far more difficult to grasp. What I was after were the crumbs, not the little white pebbles. That summer I also reread a great many romantic novels. The role that romantic novels played in shaping the sensibilities of young girls growing up in the forties is very important. And songs, the part songs played in our lives seems fundamental too."

From the floor, with her glass of manzanilla in her hand, Conchita Piquer continues to look up at me. I lean down to pick up the clipping: "Putting My Oar in on the Subject of Postwar Songs," the title reads. There is a silence.

"Is that an article of yours?" the man asks.

"Yes, it deals with the very same subject I was just speaking of. Would you like me to read it to you?"

"I'd rather hear you talk, but go ahead."

"It's just that reading it to you may help to give me some ideas, and since for the moment I'm fired with enthusiasm . . ."

"Ah, you are, are you? Good for you!"

"Yes, I'm certain that if I sat down at the typewriter right now, the words would come pouring out."

"I'll leave if you like."

"No, please, it's because you're here that things are coming to my mind."

"Well then, if you like, I'll sit myself down here on the floor, at your back, and you can begin to write."

"That wouldn't be a bad idea."

"But you should learn to write the way you talk."

"I couldn't agree more. You haven't said anything I didn't know already. But it's the most difficult thing in the world."

"Well, let's go on. Read me the article. What is it you're looking for now?"

"It's just that I don't see well without my glasses and I've no idea where I've left them."

"It seems to me I saw them over there, on top of the table. Don't you keep them in a case with a royal peacock embroidered on it?"

"Yes."

I glance over toward the table and make a move to get up, but his hand on my shoulder stops me.

"Don't bother," he says. "I'll bring them to you. Every time you go over to that table, you get all upset. And you lose the thread often enough as it is."

I see him get to his feet and walk over to the table to look for them. I notice his bony shoulders and his slightly curved back. Seen from behind like that, he looks older. He walks back over from the table. Our eyes meet. He has the glasses case in his hand.

"Don't worry, I didn't snoop at anything. These are your glasses, aren't they?"

"Yes, thanks very much."

He hands them to me. I put them on, and he sits down beside me, waiting. "The advantage of dying gray hair, apart from its dubious aesthetic value . . ." I read to myself. What an odd beginning! I'd forgotten that part. What I'm looking for must be further on. I suddenly notice that he is looking at me. I raise my eyes. There is a strange gleam in his.

"I've never seen you with glasses before," he says slowly. "Have you been wearing them for a long time?"

It is an understanding look, a look of nostalgia. On the one hand it is intriguing and almost frightening, and on the other hand rather touching.

"For four years now, it seems to me. Why?"

There is a silence that is too intense. Perhaps my eyes are gleaming as brightly as his. My last question has lingered in the air of the apartment like an echo. Why? Why? "Esperanza and Raimundo looked at each other in sad amazement." Why is he looking at me like that? In romantic novels, when you came to a scene enveloped in an atmosphere such as this one, you could bet double or nothing that the stranger was about to reveal his identity. All the descriptions that had come before—storms, mountain peaks, lonely beaches—were meant to enhance that key moment in which the man and the woman would cease to be strangers and come to know each other, or in other more thrilling versions, to recognize each other, that moment in which the famous "Do you remember?" was about to be uttered. These were invariable plot elements. They also turned up in the first serial novel that I wrote with my friend from the Institute and that we never managed to finish.

"They look very nice on you," the man says, in an unusually gentle voice.

We are now looking straight into each other's eyes without dissembling. My heart begins to race like a runaway steed. That phrase about the runaway steed also turned up frequently in those books. It is difficult to escape the literary stereotypes of one's earliest years, however hard one tries later to renounce them. I read so many romantic novels, by Eugenia Marlitt, Berta Ruck, Pérez y Pérez, Elisabeth Mulder, Duhamel. Then came Carmen de Icaza, displacing the others. She was the idol of the postwar era, introducing "moderate modernity" into the genre. The heroine might not be all that young, she might even have gray hair. She was courageous and hardworking. She had liberated herself economically, but bore the burden of a secret, tormented past.

"The telephone's ringing," the man says. "Don't you hear it?"

I stand up, alarmed. The Piquer article slides off my knees onto the floor.

"How odd! At this hour . . ."

I would like him to say, addressing me in the familiar *tú* form: "Don't answer it, stay here with me." The shift from the formal to the familiar second person form was also an extremely important moment, marking the crossing of a disquieting threshold.

"It may be for me," he says unexpectedly.

"For you?"

We look at each other once again, I from where I am standing in the doorway leading to the bedroom, he from where he is sitting, with a grave and enigmatic expression, on the sofa.

"I made the mistake of leaving this number with someone," he explains. "Or rather, I left it in a place where it might have been found. But I'm going to ask you to do something for me. Tell the person who's calling that I've already left. Will you do me that favor?"

The look we exchange is now one of complicity, more lingering than any we have thus far exchanged. I've never seen him with such a serious expression on his face. The telephone is still ringing.

"Certainly," I say.

And I go into the bedroom.

A false-bottomed valise

"How long ago has it been since I was last lying stretched out on this bed?" I wonder, as I grope about for the phone and pick up the receiver. I don't hear a thing, and switch it to the other ear. I now can hear music in the background and, closer to the phone, a hesitant breathing. I stretch out my arm and turn the light on. Todorov's book is lying on the pillow, and on top of it a little piece of paper on which I have noted: "Fantastic novel. Remember the print of Luther and the Devil. Similar atmosphere." I look in the direction of the white lacquered knickknack shelf. The place where the print is usually pinned up is empty.

A woman's voice, with a Canary Islands or an Andalusian accent, utters a distressed "hello" at the other end of the line, and then pronounces the digits of my phone number very slowly and haltingly, as though she were having trouble making them out in a nearly illegible memo book. As things stand, it was bound to be a woman.

"Yes, you have the right number."

There is a brief pause, full of suspense. It's for him, she's surely going to ask for him by name. I settle myself in a more comfortable position, the music in the background is a bolero. She's turned it down now.

"I beg your pardon, but is Alejandro there?"

I can't help smiling with that mingled surprise and joy with which we immediately accept runs of good luck when playing games. How I'd love to be able to tell my friend from the Institute what's happening after so many years. Only she could understand how amazing this is. We had made a list of the men's names we liked the most, and we hesitated for some time before choosing one for that stranger in our novel, a poet and vagabond who later turned out to be Esmeralda's cousin. They'd been childhood sweethearts who'd promised to marry each other when they grew up. One day, in the part that my friend was supposed to write, they had taken shelter from the rain in a fishermen's tavern and were looking at each other in silence, amid the smoke, hearing the music of an accordion. Suddenly Esmeralda burst into tears, and without a word the stranger took out a large handkerchief with an *A* embroidered in one corner, which she glimpsed dimly through her tears. "Álvaro? Arturo? Alejandro?" she asked herself, consumed with curiosity, as she raised it to her eyes. In the following chapter, which it was my turn to begin, all doubts were dispelled: his name was Alejandro.

"Alejandro? . . . just as I thought," I hear myself saying inadvertently.

The reply is cutting:

"Just as I thought myself."

144

I wait expectantly, fingering the note that was on top of the book. On the reverse side I read this phrase copied from it: "The time and space of supernatural life are not the time and space of daily life." No, of course they're not the same. If they were, I would wake up tomorrow on the studio couch and then would go excitedly off to school. I would tell my friend that I'd just had a great idea how to go on with the novel: "You can't possibly imagine: a mysterious woman who phones in the middle of the night; I'll tell you after class," I would whisper in her ear, and she would immediately want me to tell her more. The Religion teacher would tell us to pay attention. That was the class where we paid the least attention. He was a little short man and I could imitate him very well: "Martín Gaite, repeat what I just said."

"Tell him to come to the phone if you will."

She has said this in a somewhat defiant but at the same time anxious tone of voice. It may be that she is lying on a rumpled bed like this one, contemplating in her turn the signs of a recent bout of insomnia. I would like to see her expression, her voice alone doesn't provide enough clues. I can't imagine what her face looks like. I hesitate for a few seconds. She gives a sigh then, perhaps thinking that I've gone to call him to the phone.

"I'm sorry, but he's already left."

I regret having to lie to her, because she'll hang up immediately now and I won't be able to find out any more.

"Has it been very long since he left?"

"About ten minutes."

"Was he there very long?"

"I wouldn't have any way of knowing. Neither of us had a watch."

"What time did he arrive?"

"I can't tell you that either. . . . Is it something urgent?"

Suddenly she bursts into sobs.

"Tell me why he went to that apartment. In the name of the Virgin, tell me the truth."

"Well . . . he came to see me."

"To see you, naturally, he needed to see you again, I knew that, I told him so when he was putting his jacket on, of course you're going off to hunt up that madwoman. He slammed the door behind him as he left. I stood in the bay window shouting insults after him till he closed the front gate, I screamed at him not to come back ever again, but please tell him to forgive me, to come back. I was so angry I got carried away . . . you must understand that. . . ."

There is a silence, I can hear her agitated breathing, her sobbing. I hold my breath, torn between the irrepressible urge to delve more deeply into this disturbing story and the good sense that tells me to have nothing to do with it. The most honest thing would be to go call him and let him make up with her as best he can, but curiosity holds me back. Why can she have called me a madwoman? My only guess is that she must be confusing me with someone else. But on the other hand, I have the dizzying suspicion that I may perhaps have deserved that description. I can feel on my skin, like a stigma, that unsuspected identity, "runaway, madwoman," that has been conferred upon me. . . .

"Are you still there?" she finally asks in a pleading voice.

"Yes, I'm right here."

"Well, say something to me then."

"What do you want me to say? That I'm sorry, that he's left already, and that I . . ."

"That's not true!" she interrupts me in an even more agitated tone of voice. "You're lying to me, you said before that he was there."

"I didn't say any such thing."

"Yes, you did! I'm no fool. You said 'Just as I thought.' I heard it perfectly. What was it you thought exactly?"

Once again my mind goes back to the unfinished novel, to the fishermen's tavern, to the initial embroidered on the handkerchief. Alejandro knew who she was from their first meeting on the cliff, but he didn't tell her that till chapter five.

"Well, as it happens, I was thinking of another Alejandro," I say, without being at all certain that this is so, or that this scene and that other one are not part of the same plot.

"Ah, yes, I see!" she says sarcastically.

"I don't think you see at all, it's a very long story. But I'm afraid it wouldn't interest you."

"I don't need to have you tell it to me, I know that story already. I know everything . . . I've read the letters!"

The letters? What letters? But it's best to say nothing and let her go on. I lie there paralyzed, with my eyes fixed on the wall opposite me, hoping that the next scene will be revealed there, as though I were at the movies seeing a suspense film: the first one I ever saw in my life was called *Rebecca*. It was so famous that it became a generic name for suspense films and was also the name given to those little knitted cardigans with tiny buttons that open all the way down the front, like the one that Joan Fontaine wore in all the scenes of the movie. She would cross it over her breast in a fearful gesture, continually thinking she saw ghosts in the endless corridors of the castle of Manderley, trying in vain to get to the bottom of the mysterious story of her predecessor. The film began with an oneiric image. It was night. The camera passed through the castle gate, traveled on along a path overgrown with weeds and lined with shadowy masses of vegetation. A voice off-camera said something like: "Last night I dreamed that I was back at Manderley." The critics said it was a morbid film, for adults only, not recommended for children.

"Just as you thought, naturally!" the woman says, beside herself. "The two of you presumed I was going to call. When the telephone rang, he probably said: 'If it's her, tell her I'm not here.' He's done that to me so many times when another woman called. It's one of the many tricks in his repertoire. I'm sure he's right there next to you. . . . Alejandro, please forgive me for what happened, it was only a passing mood, Alejandro. . . ."

My good sense gets the upper hand. I sit up. This has gone too far. I must react against such nonsense. By my silent complicity I'm giving it wings, though it's also true that there is much more beauty in encouraging a mad flight of the imagination than in discouraging it by clipping its wings.

"Please, señorita, try to calm yourself and listen to me," I say in a tone of voice that I do my best to make sound serene and persuasive. "I think you're the victim of a regrettable mistake."

There is a deathly silence, the perfect markmanship of my words has downed every last one of the flock of prodigious birds flying over my head, noisily cawing "mad-mad-mad." They have fallen lifeless at my feet.

"A mistake?" she stammers. "Excuse me, but I don't understand, I'm about to go mad."

I've shut myself up in my castle again. The one who's mad is someone else. I've found a safe place once more. I think this with satisfaction and an uneasy conscience, as always happens when, after having looked down into the abyss of madness, I have managed to overcome my vertigo and take a step backward, so as to transform myself into a mere spectator of those who are drowning in that dark maelstrom. I lean down toward them, I exhort them to save themselves, stretching my hand out to them from my inaccessible balcony. I have always had ambiguous relations with madness, both attraction and repulsion, fascination and caution, that have their origins in a scene that lies far back in the past.

It is a summer morning. All of my cousins and I are in a grove of chestnuts and eucalyptus in my mother's village in Galicia. We have made a fire among some rocks. Potatoes have been put in the coals and then covered with eucalyptus leaves so that they will be impregnated with that odor as they roast. My cousins have stayed behind, turning them over every so often with a long stick, and I have gone off chasing butterflies. I have come across my father, who is sitting in a hammock a little farther on, reading a book. He asks me if the potatoes are ready yet. They were the usual appetizer in those summers, eaten with salt and washed down with a few glasses of wine. I tell him that it will be a little while longer, and he returns to his interrupted reading. It was a little leather-bound book, one of the ones in the "Crisol" collection, with a red silk ribbon for a place marker. As I sat there on the ground I looked up at the title, written on the spine in gilt letters: *The Praise of Folly*. I reread it incredulously. I found it incomprehensible that my father, on whose lips the word mad always had a clearly pejorative ring to it, should be absorbed in that text with a beatific smile on his face. I didn't dare ask him anything. The peace of those surroundings became enigmatic. The chestnut-brown butterflies fluttering about in spirals had impenetrable eyes on their wings. The silence closed in about us, stifling and disturbing. "What an odd title, isn't it, papa?" I finally dared say. And he looked at me as though he had just waked up, as though he had been caught *in flagrante*. The following winter he showed me, one afternoon, the portrait of Erasmus of Rotterdam that occupied a place of honor in his study. He told me that he was a very great and wise man, and that only minds as lucid as his can set themselves up as judges of madness and see even its positive aspects, though this is a delicate and perilous under-taking.

"Please, tell me something. . . ." the broken, faltering voice at the other end of the line says. "Does your name by any chance begin with the letter *C*?"

"Yes . . . but what does that have to do with anything?"

I have given a start. The mauve-colored spirals in the wall-paper begin to turn round and round, forming the hieroglyph once again. I am kneeling on the beach, as in the beginning, drawing on the sand, with the *C* of my name, a house, a bedroom, and a bed. What strange flashbacks keep occurring in the plot of this story, or can it be that it has never moved ahead except in my imagination?

"And do you sometimes sign things with just your initial?"

"Yes, sometimes, but . . ."

"Aha, I knew it all the time, don't you see that there's no mistake? A big *C,* almost always with a dot after it, written with a slight slant. That's a sign of defiance."

"Defiance?"

"Yes. I have a friend, you see, who's a graphologist, and last year she gave me a book where it says that about capital letters that have a period after them and are slanted. I wanted to study graphology for the express purpose of understanding him from his handwriting when I began to notice that he was acting strangely toward me. But he laughs at everything I set out to study, he says it's because I have a secret urge to create complications, that I don't know what I want, that I get tired of things immediately, that's what he says, but it's because he discourages me. He's gradually destroyed me, taking all my hopes away, one by one. You don't know him, he's a male chauvinist."

"A male chauvinist? . . . He didn't strike me as one."

"It's horrible to fall in love like that," she says, sounding utterly dejected all of a sudden, as though she hasn't heard me, "to spend your life thinking of nothing but doing things to interest a man so he won't stop loving you, it doesn't get you anywhere. They notice and they despise you for it, there's no way around it. Hasn't that ever happened to you?"

I am touched by her hopeless tone of voice, but getting involved in an exchange of confidences doesn't interest me. I prefer not to climb down from my balcony.

"Well, my dear, we've all been through some bad moments, but we have to try to pull ourselves together."

I'm immediately ashamed of the uselessness of my counsel, formulated in the language of an Advice to the Lovelorn column, in that aseptic and escapist tone of *Y* magazine. Hence her indignant answer is like the gypsy's insult flung in the face of the churl. I feel I've deserved it.

"How can you know what real passion is!"

It almost makes me laugh. It sounds like the words of one of Conchita Piquer's songs. Yet despite the fact that these female fits of jealousy have lost, with the passage of time, the magic aura of popularity that once surrounded them and the fact that I myself have made fun of them so many times, the bitter taste that made those songs something special, a taste that her words have revived on the palate of memory, is something I respect. In the anaesthetized postwar world, between servings of that compote of words and music—carefully cooked up and dished out in turn by the composers of boleros and the comrades of the Women's Section—to lull engaged couples being herded toward a marriage without problems, to shore up beliefs and bring beatific smiles to people's lips, a dark wind sometimes came up unexpectedly, in the voice of Conchita Piquer, in the stories her songs told. Stories of girls who were not at all like the ones we knew, who were never going to enjoy the tender affection of the peaceable home and fireside that set us respectable young ladies to dreaming—

girls drifting on the fringes of society, unprotected by the law. These women had no first or last names. They filed past with no identity, involved in conflicts stemming from their not having one, aggressively raising their nicknames as a shield to protect themselves: Lily, Gypsy, Nightingale, the Fifteen Thousand Peseta Girl. They had provocative and defenseless bodies, and as the finishing touch, beautiful faces with dark circles under the eyes. Through all the different rumors and conflicting versions, the song tried to track down the reason for those dark circles. There were those who said yes, others who said no. Why does she dress in black if nobody's died? Where does she go so early in the morning with her little face yellower than straw? But nobody knew the real reason for the anguish that was consuming her. It was hard to imagine those sections of the city, slums and cheap cafés through which these girls aimlessly wandered in anonymous dishonor, the lodgings and rooms in which they holed up, yet one felt that they were much more creatures of flesh and blood than those other pairs of lovers in the boleros who swore in the moonlight to love each other forever. In these stories of Conchita's, the light of the moon shone down only on betrayals, stabbings, cheap kisses, tears of rage and fear. A rhetoric that today is trite and stale, but that in those days was meant to serve as a revulsive, as an undermining of the foundations of happiness that the propagandists of hope endeavored to reinforce. Those women who staggered through life and did not bid their intended goodnight at their front door at 9:30 on the dot made people uneasy, because they hinted at the existence of a world where fidelity and eternal values had not won the day. They were the rubble left by the war. They exposed to view that emptiness that lay all about, so hard to hide, that muffled atmosphere, like the one that presides over sickbeds, when one's every move is made amid prohibitions, cautiously, and with a feeling of being entirely out of place. Nobody wanted to speak of the cataclysm that had just torn the country apart, but the bandaged wounds still throbbed, though no moans or shots could be heard. It was an artificial silence, an emptiness that there was an urgent need to fill with anything whatsoever. People had stopped talking of Robledo de Chavela, of the valiant and loyal legionnaire, of the gunners that the artillery regiment is calling to their posts to man the cannons. They had now latched onto tender sentiments, and were peddling patience and hope.

> *Yo sé esperar*
> *como espera la noche a la luz*
> *como esperan las flores*
> *que el rocío les envuelva . . .**

one bolero said.

Waiting was the key word, patient waiting was the trump suit. And we learned to wait, not thinking that the wait would turn out to be such a long one. We waited inside our houses, in the heat of the brazier, in our back rooms, amid cheap toys and textbooks that showed us the haughty likenesses of Cardinal Cisneros and Queen Isabella, with sweets

*I know how to wait / as the night waits for the light / as the flowers wait / for the dew to envelop them. *(Translator's note.)*

rationed, listening to talk about *estraperlo*—which was no longer a sort of roulette that has two colors, *le blanc et le rouge*—listening to the radio, decorating our dreams with the material that those songs supplied us with, lulled by the sound of their words of hope. At afternoon snack time, we broke off our studies of ungulates, of the clerical verse form of the Middle Ages, or of the conquest of the New World, to sit around the radio and listen, as we watched the sun set, to the soft, sweet boleros of Bonet de San Pedro, of Machín, or of Raúl Abril. And then a sudden violent gust of wind swept away the sweetness and roiled the hope: "E.A.J. 56, Radio Salamanca. You are about to hear 'Tatuaje,' sung by Conchita Piquer." That was something else, that was telling a real story, one recalled by a woman of ill fame, wandering from one bar counter to another, doomed to search forever for that soldier with hair as blond as beer who had the name of a woman tattooed on his chest and who had left a forgotten kiss on her lips as they parted. He was in love with another, with that woman whose name he had engraved forever on his skin, and she knew it. It was a hopeless search, but that forgotten kiss of the sailor who went away, remembered as she sat in front of a glass of brandy in the bars down along the harbor, facing the light of dawn, was transformed, in the rough voice of Conchita Piquer, into something absolutely real and tangible, into an eternal talisman of love. A passion such as that was forbidden us sensible, decent young ladies of the new Spain.

"Listen, please . . . you haven't hung up, have you?" the upset voice of this woman goes on. *She* at least seems to know what passion is.

"No."

"I couldn't help wondering, since you aren't saying anything."

"It's just that I don't know what to say."

"I don't really know what I'm saying either. Excuse me, I must be boring you. It's very hard to explain over the phone, and there are so many things I'd like to tell you. I realize that this hour of the night is hardly the right time though. But let me ask you to do me just one favor before you hang up on me. . . ."

"I have no intention of hanging up on you. You can say whatever you like."

"Wow, whatever I like! But that's impossible, we'd never get to the end, and you have to get your sleep."

"Don't worry about it, I sleep very little. I suffer from insomnia."

"Yes, I already knew that. All the letters begin by saying that it's late at night or in the wee hours of the morning and that you can't sleep. . . ."

"Wait a second, I'm getting all mixed up."

"Well, so am I. . . . I haven't read even a quarter of them and I'm already all confused. Do you know the feeling you get when you start wandering through one of those mazes at fairgrounds? Well, it's like that. The moment he'd gone, I went upstairs to the cubbyhole. He'd taken them out of the trunk and put them somewhere else. He's often quite distrustful, and what's more he'd locked the door. I had to get in through the skylight on the roof. Do you know where he'd hidden them? Under the mattress. The storm caught me up

there and I was scared stiff he'd come back. What an afternoon, my dear, it'll sound straight out of a detective story if
I tell you."

"Do tell me, please, but in a little more orderly way, if you
can."

"I don't know if I'll be able to, my way of explaining things
is just as they happen to come to mind. But first of all, promise me you'll do me a favor."

"If I can," I say guardedly, intuiting that there's slippery
ground ahead.

"Watch your step," an inner voice warns me. "Control your
curiosity. Curiosity has always gotten you into terrible messes
where you lose your footing and it's no use to try to cling to
the bars of your balustrade."

"Come on, don't be such a Galician," she says in an impatient voice.

"How do you know I'm a Galician?"

"I didn't know, I just happened to say that, for no reason at
all. Don't take it as an insult, it's just that in Puerto Real we
always say that to people who beat around the bush. *He* takes
it as an insult, but I really don't have anything against
Galicia. Certain things are just a custom. In my town the
minute anybody asks a favor of you, you answer "It's done,"
then and there, and afterwards if you can you do it and if you
can't never mind, it doesn't matter. Being cautious just isn't
my way. Do you want me to walk straight into the lion's den?
Well here I am, already inside it. Anyway, don't worry, the
favor I'm about to ask of you is no big deal."

"It doesn't matter," I say, setting aside my fear of walking straight into the lion's den and feeling at the same time that I'm already inside it. "What's the favor? It's done."

"Thanks. All I wanted to ask of you is not to tell him I've read the letters. He'd never forgive me. He had them hidden away like a treasure, and of course the more people hide things from you the more they arouse your curiosity, that's only natural. The quarrel this afternoon . . ."

"What letters is it you're talking about?" I interrupt.

My voice has sounded like a muffled cry to me. There's no getting round it, I'm beginning to lose my footing.

"The quarrel this afternoon," she goes on, "started precisely on account of that, because he found me in the cubbyhole snooping in the trunk. I didn't hear him coming, he must have sneaked upstairs on tiptoe. I turned as white as a sheet, I swear. When I looked around and saw him there behind me with a face as stern as a judge's, there I was, kneeling on the floor with the trunk open in front of me and no possible way of hiding what I was up to. 'What are you doing?' he said with a sudden look in his eyes that was really scary. He's given me strict orders not to go up to the cubbyhole when he's not there."

"Well, I must say, it sounds straight out of the story of Bluebeard," I comment, trying to joke with her.

"Exactly. You hit the nail right on the head. It so happens I call him Bluebeard when he comes on like that. I told him I hadn't seen anything but he didn't swallow that lie. He grabbed me by the hair and pulled me up off the floor, and I started trembling. I knew he was going to beat me."

"And did he?"

"Sure he did, and it wasn't the first time. What I've gone through these last few months is like a gypsy song."

"It sounds incredible."

"I know it does, dearie, but you don't know him. You were right when you said before that the Alejandro you were talking about was somebody else entirely. I've caught on that he's been all sweetness and light with you. Anyway, what saved me was that he'd put the letters back where he usually kept them and didn't dare feel the lining of the valise in front of me, because if he had that would have given him away. I'd already figured out that it was a valise with a false bottom."

"How odd! Do valises with false bottoms still exist today?"

"Well, this one does, that's for sure."

"It must have belonged to one of his grandfathers."

"I haven't the faintest idea whose valise it may have been, or where the devil he came across it. He brought it back here after he went to settle the whole business about his father's inheritance, but that's another long story. It's one with a curse on it, since they're all about to come to blows over it. Naturally I couldn't care less. I don't want to have anything to do with any of them. So what if they all take me for a lousy bitch? So much the worse for them, but what they don't have any right to say is that I'm with Alejandro because I'm interested in his money, if you get what I mean. When I first met him I didn't know who his family was or anything and if it wasn't for me he'd have died of starvation, and the only thing that mattered was that we loved each other, that was the best time of all, and damn that dough."

Yes, the whole story was like a gypsy song:

Maldito parné
que por tu culpita
perdí yo al gitano
que fue mi querer . . . *

Money was often mentioned in those songs, almost always to curse it, to warn against the misfortunes it brings with it. Wealth and love were pictured as irreconcilable concepts. The same thing happened in romantic novels: almost without exception, it was the disinherited who possessed generous and unselfish souls.

"The father," she goes on, "was an absolute madman, but he at least was better than the others. He never blamed me for anything. I think he was even grateful to me because Alejandro had sort of pulled himself together when he was with me. I had hardly any dealings with the man. He had a terrible temper. He was a really odd character, that's for sure. He went hunting one afternoon and was found dead in the woods. They say his shotgun went off accidentally, but who knows? He was living with a young girl and she was cheating on him. Well anyway, you probably know all that already."

"No, I didn't know anything about it."

"You must have known. It was a very strange death, and it was in all the papers."

---

*Goddamned dough / it was all your fault / that I lost the gypsy / who was my love . . . *(Translator's note.)*

"I hardly ever read the papers. But go on with the business about the valise. He brought it back, and then what happened?"

"Nothing, except that that's when all our troubles began. But my hunches usually turn out to be right and I had my suspicions about that valise. Can you believe it? The moment I saw it in his hand when he came back from that damned trip to Galicia. I'd gone to the station to meet him. I was wearing a green dress that's a favorite of his, and the minute he got off the train, wham, a bucketful of cold water. I should leave him alone. Why had I come to the station? You can't imagine the fuss he made as we were waiting for the taxi because I happened to ask him where he'd gotten that valise and picked it up for a minute to carry it for him. 'It's not a bit heavy. Is this all the baggage you have with you?' I say to him and he grabs it away from me in a rage. Who'd given me permission to touch it, I was always trying to stick my nose in other people's business, and he wouldn't even let the taxi driver take it. He just sat there with it between his legs the whole time, hanging on to it for dear life, as though somebody might try to steal it, and not saying one word to me. But since I hadn't done anything to him and since I know what he's like, I thought: 'The best thing to do is to take it as a joke, Carola. If you pick a fight with him you're lost.' And I say to him: 'Listen, if this little valise is all you've brought back with you, that's some inheritance, darling. It's worth about as much as the one Puss-in-Boots got as his share in the fairy tale.' I thought it would make him laugh and that would be the end of his being so mad at me. Wouldn't you have laughed?"

"Yes, it's very funny."

"Well, he didn't think it was the least bit funny. He looked at me as though he didn't know me, not even with hatred in his eyes, because hatred is something else again. I prefer it a thousand times over. The worst thing is when they look at you like that, as though you were just an old shoe. An icy look, that's the first hint that there's another woman. It's a dead giveaway. By the way, I'm going to ask you a question, as though you were a real friend. Weren't you by chance in Galicia around that time?"

Dates, the little white pebbles. Let's see if we manage to get out of this tangled forest by following the trail of the little white pebbles.

"When was it exactly? Tell me the precise date."

"That's true, I haven't told you. Wait a minute till I figure out just when it was. His father died in June, didn't he?"

"I've no idea."

"In June, that's right. So the trip, the one when he brought back the valise, must have been around the end of the summer, about six months or so ago."

"I see. . . ." I say disappointedly, looking at the quotation from Todorov.

Nothing clicks; the dates don't coincide: "The time and space of supernatural life are not the time and space of daily life." It's obvious that tonight little white pebbles merely serve to compound the confusion.

"No, I'm sorry. I remember very well that the last time I was in Galicia was in the summer of '73."

"Well, anyhow, it doesn't matter. I'd already figured out that it all had to do with a story that went much further back. And I was all the more jealous for that very reason. Why wouldn't I have poked around in the valise? Put yourself in my shoes. Being with a man who sits staring into space for hours on end and knowing that there's something in his past that he's never going to tell you about is unbearable. It's torture."

I remember Joan Fontaine again, unable to get to sleep in that immense old mansion at Manderley, lying with her eyes wide open in the dark. I hear that voice off-camera that sounded even deeper and more solemn as it echoed off the vaulted ceiling, repeating bits of conversations that gave her clues about her mysterious predecessor: "Her name was Rebecca de Winters, everyone says that she was very beautiful, that her husband adored her. . . ."

"Naturally the remedy was worse than the sickness, seeing that the letters aren't dated. . . ."

"There's no date on any of them?"

"No, she heads them 'Friday night,' or 'Sunday, four in the morning,' and sometimes there's not even that. And the worst of it is that you read them and there are no concrete details of any sort. It's as though they were out of a book. They're also a way of trying to make the time pass. I don't care what he says."

"But what *does* he say?"

I'm furious at myself for beginning to ask her questions. It's the wrong tack to take.

"Well, he's always been very fond of books you never really understand. We have very different tastes in that respect, and what's more, ever since I first met him he keeps saying, 'Why is it that people don't write love letters the way they used to?'

And as a matter of fact, when he was in Galicia I wrote him two or three times, but he didn't answer me. The thing is I don't know what to say. I have a terribly hard time writing letters and it's even worse if they're love letters. It always seems to me as though you're trying to put something over on somebody. About a month ago, he brought the subject up again. My cousin Rafael was here too at the time and he said that I was the one who was right, and Alejandro looked at us as though he were miles above us in the clouds, smiling to himself so scornfully it made my blood run cold: 'How would the two of you know what a love letter is!' It was at that very moment that I got the idea in my head that there were letters from another woman in the valise. I had thought at first that what was inside it were papers having to do with the inheritance, though it seemed odd to store something as valuable as that up there in that cubbyhole. But I'm getting you all mixed up, isn't that so?"

"Well, yes, as a matter of fact. . . ."

"Where was I?"

"You were telling about the taxi trip, when he wouldn't talk to you."

"Oh, yes, and he went on like that, not saying a word to me. I finally didn't even look at him out of the corner of my eye — a silly fight, the kind where you don't even know why you're angry — and when we arrived at the house he said he didn't have any change and got out clutching the suitcase for dear life, in such a hurry that even the taxi driver thought it was odd, and said to me: 'Hey, dearie, what's eating your boyfriend?' A dark-haired young man, very handsome. And already half in tears, I say to him: 'That's what I'd like to know.' Because, you know, no matter how bad you're feeling, if somebody asks you something in a polite way, you aren't going to leave them up in the air without answering something. But then right away he began to say that I was worth a thousand times more than my friend was, the usual sort of thing, and I realized that he was trying to make out with me and cut him short: 'I'm sorry, but you've picked the wrong day.' That was a dumb thing to say, you know, it's like Silvia said to me the next day: 'You sure are stupid, what you should have done was go off with the taxi driver and not come back for three days. You're not even the shadow of your former self.' And how right she was. Once upon a time I had the world on a string. Silvia's my friend the graphologist."

"Ah, I see."

"Anyway, I followed him into the villa and I didn't see him anywhere. I called and called him. I was so upset I didn't know what to do, but then finally I said to myself: 'Maybe he's gone up to the cubbyhole,' because every time he gets some wild idea into his head he shuts himself up there. It's a mania of his I just don't understand. He might at least let me fix it up for him. Of course, as Silvia says, if you fix it up for him it'll be worse. That'll give him an excuse not to ever come downstairs and spend time with you, because he's used to having other people solve all his problems for him, and what's more his handwriting shows that he's somewhat schizophrenic. I climb up the stairs and in fact he was just shutting the door as I got there. I say to him: 'What's the matter with you, Alejandro, what is it I've done to you?' And he's slamming the door in my face: 'Get out of the way. Can't you see I can't get the door closed with you standing there?' And there was nothing I could do. Anyhow, to make a long story short so as not to bore you, he's practically lived up there ever since that day, shut up like a cockroach with the famous valise, in that dingy little room just off the attic, with nothing in it except a cot and four pieces of broken-down furniture. Do you get the picture? Lately he's taken books, a lamp, and an armchair up there. Don't tell me that's normal behavior. He could have fixed up any other room for himself, what with all the empty ones there are in this downstairs part of the house overlooking the garden, don't you agree?"

"Well, that's something very personal. Perhaps the cubbyhole seems like a cozier place to him. I can't say. I don't know the house."

"What do you mean you don't know the house? It's the old villa built in the twenties in Ciudad Lineal, where his sister used to live. Weren't you a friend of his sister's?

"What sister are you talking about?"

"About Laura, the married one. Anyway, that's what I supposed, since María Antonia's been in Caracas for twenty years. I don't imagine you've ever lived in Caracas."

"No, I've never been to Caracas."

"Well then, it has to be Laura."

"And what makes you say I must have been a friend of hers?"

"Come on, I haven't said any such thing. How should I know? All I'm saying is that she may be the one who was with you when the two of you found Alejandro at the end of that passageway."

"A passageway? I don't understand a word of what you're saying."

"Yes, a passageway. A sort of spiral ramp that went up and up with lots of turns. You tell about it in a letter. The two of you were following a man who lighted your way with a lantern, and then you came out into the open air, and there he was, lying on the ground amid some trees, with a cat on top of his chest. You knelt down at his side and heard him speaking in a strange tongue. . . ."

"But all of this is most peculiar."

"Yes, that's because it was a dream, but a person doesn't realize that till the end. Of course you write whatever comes into your head and it's hard to make heads or tails of much of anything. Lots of the letters are dreams, most of them in fact. Incidentally, I'm beginning to put two and two together now. He always asked me, when we woke up, what I'd dreamed and seemed disappointed whenever I answered 'Nothing.' The thing is, I sleep like a log. Do you dream a lot?"

"Yes, a lot, but there's almost never time enough to write my dreams down and I can't tell them to anybody. That's what I find the most distressing."

"Well, it's a thorn you've definitely removed from your flesh now, dearie, there's no doubt of that."

I'm aware that I've been lost for some time now, but keep circling back to the same spot trying to orient myself.

"Tell me one thing though: how do you know that I was the one who wrote those letters?"

"When I found them underneath the mattress, they had a piece of paper on top of them with your telephone number written on it in red. He knows I'm consumed with curiosity. He must have left it there as bait in order to know whether I'd read the letters. I've been hesitating whether to phone you or not. I called to feel out the terrain, but don't get the idea that I was certain, when I called, that you were the one who'd written them."

"And now?"

"I'm not sure now either. . . . And would you like me to tell you something?'

"Yes."

"I can't decide one way or the other any more. I'm all the way inside the lion's den."

There is a silence. She seems to be searching for a way to explain herself.

"I don't know, something very strange is happening to me. It's as though I weren't sure either than you really exist, the woman of the letters, I mean. . . . At first, when I heard your voice it almost. . . . It's awful. . . ."

"It almost what? Say whatever you like."

"It almost scared me."

Giving a name to feelings is an infallible way of making them take on reality. Fear had been buzzing about the room for some time, but I hadn't seen it, and now it's right here, just above my face, the blue-bottle fly of fear, and there is only one means of chasing it away: stop defending myself, confront the temptation that is threatening me. I close my eyes, dig my fingernails into Todorov's book.

"May I ask you a favor?"

"Yes, of course, woman. It's done.'

"Read me some of those letters."

How much I wanted to ask her to do that! It's as though I'd opened the window so that the blue-bottle fly could get out, while at the same time running the risk, of course, that another one would fly in.

"All right, but you'll have to wait a little while, because I'll have to go out onto the roof again and climb in through the skylight. Luckily he's cleared out for the moment."

I think vaguely that this is too much, that if I told all this to my friend in class, the two of us would take off out the window, the one with the dirty panes, hand in hand, beneath the astonished gaze of the Religion teacher. "But where in the world can those two girls have gone flying off to?" he'd ask with his mouth gaping open. "Go chase after them, they've got the devil in the flesh." There is a point where fantastic literature crosses over the threshold of the marvelous, and from then on everything is possible and believable. We are flying through the air as in one of Lewis Carroll's stories, soaring above the rooftops of a city. It is nighttime and my friend keeps a tight hold on my hand and laughs with her hair all mussed, because it's very windy. "Look," I say to her, "you're now going to see a woman crawling on all fours over the roof tiles and making her way inside through that skylight." "How great," she says. "Tell me more."

"Unless you'd rather I phoned you back."

"No, I'd rather wait for you."

"Okay. I'll be right back."

I hear the sound of the receiver being put down, and the silence round about me suddenly makes me feel panicky when

I remember that the man in black is really there outside my bedroom, just a few steps away—that is to say, I presume that he's still there. I am torn between the desire to peek out and see and the fear of changing position. He may have turned into some frightful animal: a dragon, a werewolf. He may even have disappeared. I lie there paralyzed, my gaze riveted on the red curtain. The most terrible thing would be for him to appear in my room all of a sudden looking at me with Bluebeard eyes, but of course he wouldn't do that, how absurd. He'd ask first: "May I come in?" Only a little while ago he assured me that he'd never entered a woman's bedroom without her consent—even though it is also true that the image of him that this girl from Puerto Real is tracing for me has very little to do with that aloof, refined person with whom I was discussing the game of Red Light. The thing that's most exciting is contradictory versions. They're the very basis of literature. We are not just one being, but many, exactly as real history is not what is written by putting dates in their proper order and then presenting it to us as a single whole. Each person who has seen us or spoken to us at a certain time retains one piece of the puzzle that we will never be able to see all put together. My image shatters and is refracted in infinite reflections. I am flying above the rooftops hand in hand with a friend who is dead now, and at the same time I am walking along a passageway alongside the sister of the man in black, a woman I haven't the least memory of. Of course that was a dream, but it is a dream that at some moment I must have dreamed, perhaps lying in this very same bed from which I am now gazing at the red curtain with my nerves all on edge, waiting to hear once again the voice that has brought me these unfinished stories, avidly waiting for her to tell me the end of them. What a long time it's taking her. On the other end of the line is a silent receiver, abandoned on top of some piece of furniture. What can the room it's in be like? I need to imagine what it looks like so as to fill in some way or other this time spent waiting. She has said that it's an old villa in Ciudad Lineal that I'm familiar with. I've never been inside any old villa in Ciudad Lineal, not that I wouldn't have liked very much to see the inside of one. I've often strolled around in that part of town, once upon a time just inside the city limits, looking at those villas from the outside, years ago especially, when they threatened to tear down the handsomest ones. There are probably very few of them left standing now. I remember very well one that has now disappeared, one that I prowled around one autumn afternoon. It was beautiful. It had a watchtower and dry leaves on the stairs. A dog came out of it all of a sudden, rushed over to the gate, and began to bark furiously at me. That scene was the germ of my novel *Ritmo Lento*. If I hadn't seen that house I wouldn't have written it.

I'm numb all over. I rise silently to my feet and take a few steps toward the radiator. I recognize the various objects that spilled out all over the floor when I dropped the sewing box, before the man in black arrived. I don't see the letter on blue paper. Perhaps I put it away somewhere else, or it may be that I took it out of the room, like the print of Luther, but I'm not going to let that problem prey on my mind. We're in the middle of another story now, another search, though who knows if it's really a different one; everything is related tonight. I lean on the radiator to kill time. I don't dare peek out through the curtain. I sense that that would ruin everything — be quiet, be patient. I look at the large picture hanging above the bed, it shows some dark trees peeking out above a wall, and in the distance is a train. The painted time flows, overflows the frame, the light appears to be that of the break of day.

After some time, which has seemed to me to be more than sufficient, I walk back over to the bed on tiptoe, settle down in a comfortable position on top of the bedclothes that have retained the imprint of my body, pick up the telephone and listen again. I can hear sounds on the other end of the line now.

"Hello, are you there?" I ask.

She doesn't answer me, apparently she's talking to someone. Or can she have turned the radio on? No, the murmur becomes less confused, I can make out her voice now, counterpointed by another one, a male voice. They are arguing. All I can catch are disjointed phrases. She has just said, "Leave me alone." The scene — I need to have a setting for it — is taking place in the fictitious room that I invented and decorated for *Ritmo Lento,* thanks to my having seen a real setting, the study where David Fuente's father worked. There was a divan upholstered in worn velvet, a large bookcase and a corner fireplace, the design of the wallpaper was a dull red flower pattern, the window overlooked the garden behind the villa, with a greenhouse. As long as I live, that room continues to exist and I use it as a way of orienting myself, even though it's a product of my imagination and even though they've torn down that villa that I saw with the dog barking. What difference does that make—the back room also continues to exist and has been rescued from death, even though they've torn down the building on the Plaza de los Bandos. Last year a friend sent me a clipping from *El Adelanto* mentioning it.

The voices have grown louder now, closer at hand. "Please, Carola, don't be mean. What's it to you?" the man says. It's true, her name is Carola, she's told me so before. All of a sudden I have a brilliant idea: the letters are signed with a *C*. What if she wrote them herself and doesn't remember that she did? She has the impression that she's never liked writing letters, much less love letters, but she may be mistaken. What does anybody ever know about himself or herself? Life is so full of surprises . . .

"Leave me alone, I've already told you that I'm not talking to him, that it's a girlfriend of mine. . . . You don't know her. . . . Wait for me in the other room, I'll be through right away." Of this sentence, that I have heard very clearly and distinctly, it is the last words above all that stick in my mind. They have been like a dagger thrust, like that strange presentiment that unexpectedly creeps into one's dreams, arousing the suspicion that they are but insubstantial dreams, warning that the moment of awakening is close at hand. "I'll be through right away." It's awful. She's not going to have time to read me the letters.

"Well, if you insist. You're really such a pest, you know, but only for a little while, and then you're to leave."

"All right," the man's voice says submissively, very close now.

And I immediately hear the sound of the receiver being picked up from wherever it's lying. I remember now that in

David Fuente's father's study there was no telephone. It can't be that room. The divan, the red wallpaper, the bookcase vanish. It's a room I've never been in, I can't see a thing, I'm bumping into blank walls.

"Alejandro?" the man's voice says on the phone. "Is that you?"

"I don't understand what's going on," I answer. "Where is Carola? I was talking to her. Who are you?"

"And who are *you?*"

"A friend of Carola's."

I now hear the sound of her voice. She may have grabbed the phone out of his hand.

"Come off it, Rafael, aren't you satisfied that it's a woman? What are you trying to do, take down all her vital statistics? Go on, close the door. Out with you, I'll be there in just a minute."

She ends that exchange with an impatient sigh, which I take it is meant for my ears. I then hear the sound of a door slamming.

"Whew, so much the better! Are you still there?" she says into the phone.

"Yes, but what's going on?"

"Nothing, dearie, I'm sorry, but I'm going to have to leave you. I don't know what possesses us when it comes to men. We women never learn."

"Well, never mind. Did you bring the letters to read to me?"

"Heavens no, impossible. The thing is that Rafael's turned up, everything's one big mess tonight."

I am unable to contain my indignation.

"You told me you were going to bring them down to me. You shouldn't have told me that," I protest with the stubbornness of a child who's been cheated out of an eagerly awaited toy. "Is that the way people in Puerto Real keep promises? If so, it would be better if they didn't promise all the things they do."

"Don't be angry, woman, I too was enjoying talking with you. I'd even gotten over the bad mood I was in, and I hope you haven't taken it into your head that I'm looking forward to having to put up with Rafael, who on top of everything else has come here to reproach me for all sorts of things, when I didn't even remember what his damned name was."

"Well then, tell him to go away."

"I can't, not when I was the one who phoned him to come over, don't you see? I asked him to come and console me, I was beaten to a pulp. . . ."

"But when was that?"

"Before I called you. I naturally thought: 'It's pretty likely he won't turn up, since I do such awful things to him and only call on him when I'm in some sort of trouble . . . but it's hopeless, the worse I treat him, the more faithful he is, and the more faithful he is, the worse I treat him. I realize now that that's the way things are bound to turn out."

"Well then, don't complain," I say, suddenly bored with the whole affair now that I see that my role in the drama has come to an end.

"That's life for you, when all is said and done we like it that somebody else suffers on our account, and the righteous always pay for the sinners. Doesn't it seem that way to you?"

"How should I know!" I answer ill-humoredly, not wanting to receive a rosary of cheap bits of philosophy as the only reward for my long wait.

"But please don't be angry, I'm really sorry not to have been able to bring the letters down to you."

"I'm even sorrier."

"Anyway, it would have been risky. Just think what would have happened if Alejandro had come back all of a sudden and caught me up there again. Heaven help me, I don't even want to think about it. Even though I don't imagine that he'll be coming back at this late hour, right? Didn't he tell you where he was going?"

"He didn't say anything to me, but anyway, what does it matter to you? Don't worry so much about him, it's quite obvious that you've got company now."

"Really and truly, it makes me furious to have to leave you like this. . . ."

"Never mind, what does it matter anyway!"

"Well, all right, I won't bore you any longer. Thanks for everything."

"Think nothing of it. Good night," I say curtly.

I wait a few seconds before hanging up. She does the same, as though she were trying to think of something to say to apologize for her abrupt farewell.

"I'd like it if you were the one in the letters," she finally murmurs shyly.

"I'd like to be her too," I say with a sigh. "Let's hope I was."

And I hang up immediately, without adding a single word more, ashamed of having confessed such a thing to a stranger.

The island of bergai

I walk over to the doorway, without a sound, and peek my head out, hiding behind the curtain as though I were observing, from the wings, the stage set where I shall be making my entrance in just a moment. I recognize it, it's the same one as before. I see the table with the pile of sheets of paper underneath the hat — the prop man has plainly added a few more — and in the background, through the opening at stage right (presuming that the orchestra seats are located on the terrace), I glimpse the black and white tiles of the hallway that leads to the rest of the apartment. The doorway is half concealed by a red velvet curtain that matches the one I'm hiding behind, but it isn't moving, and no form is visible behind it. One does not have the impression that a new actor is going to make his appearance from that side of the stage. The character dressed in black is all ready to begin, he is calmly sitting on the sofa awaiting my entrance onstage. Everything suggests that the two of us are going to go on with our scene together. He is pretending to be absorbed in reading some newspaper clippings, but what he is really doing is going over his part, whereas I've forgotten mine entirely. The minute I realize this I'm overcome with a sudden loss of nerve that takes the form of two physical symptoms: I feel weak in the knees and sick to my stomach. I steal furtively back into the bedroom, sit down in a low chair upholstered in yellow in front of the dressing table, and lean on my elbows facing the long mirror, as I search for something in my memory, which has suddenly turned into a fallow field. What was it I was supposed to say to him? I don't remember one thing, I question that pale countenance before me in vain, for the only thing it reflects is my own stupor.

And all of a sudden a strange transformation takes place. The expression on the face is the same, but it is now surrounded by a lace coif, and the dark circles under the eyes and the tiny wrinkles around them have disappeared. Moreover, the mirror has now become a smaller, oval one, and the walls of the dressing room have bare patches where the paint has peeled off. I look, my mind a blank, at one shaped like a fish. My head is reeling. That bare patch is the only thing that exists. I hear sounds of confusion outside. From behind me, a frail girl dressed as a sixteenth-century noblewoman comes rushing across the room toward me. "Whatever are you doing? We're waiting for you. Come on, Agustín's already onstage." "I've forgotten everything, Conchita, it's awful, I can't go out there." "Don't talk nonsense, come on, it's always like that the first time. The minute you make your entrance you remember immediately. Can I give you a bit of advice? Put a little more eye makeup on. When you see how pretty you look you'll feel more confident." I grab a black eye-pencil that's lying on the dressing table and carefully outline my eyes, the way I did that first time I trod the boards of the Teatro Liceo in Salamanca, in a performance of a one-act farce by Cervantes. The lace coif has now disappeared, but so has my nervousness. All I need remember is that we were a great success. Among the papers that I burned years ago, I seem to remember that there was a highly laudatory review from *El Adelanto,* predicting a glorious future for me as an actress. I was in my second year at the university. I stand up and walk back over to the curtain. The only thing I can do is make as fearless and as serene an entrance as possible.

The man in black is still there. I pluck up my courage by telling myself that after all, despite the studied calm with which he is prepared to receive me, he has no notion of the new facts I have just learned about him. I know that he is capable of beating a woman and that his handwriting reveals a certain tendency toward schizophrenia. Not that I am thinking of making use of these things I've learned except as a last resort, but they are a protection of my position, as is always true of the secret tricks one holds in a card game. In the last analysis, everything is a game, and success depends on one's ability to concentrate. I must keep that firmly in mind, remember that our nerves get the better of us when we lose sight of the game itself by turning our attention to the rules laid down for it beforehand. What difference does it make, let him put whatever he wants to on the program. Programs have never been of any use for anything. What I have to do is wait for him to speak first, keep a close eye on the changes of expression on his face as they follow one upon the other, pay attention to the variations in the lines he speaks, listen to him calmly. That will be enough for me to come up with a brilliant improvised speech in reply. I stand there a few moments more, feeling relaxed and secure, knowing that he is unaware that I'm spying on him. Then I put on my glasses, which I have been carrying in my hand, draw back the curtain, and come striding resolutely onstage. I am surprised that there was not a burst of applause greeting my entrance.

He does not raise his eyes, he is reading my article on Conchita Piquer. It's better that way, there's no hurry. In the theater silences count as much as the text, they create the tension necessary to involve the spectator in the plot, and a good actor must know how to wait out these pauses impassively, to fill them with his mere presence. I kneel down, and endeavoring to make my gestures as graceful as possible, I begin to pick up the papers that fell to the floor in the previous act and place them one by one in the beige folder. When I've finished, I rise to my feet and put the folder back in the left-hand drawer, which is still open. The first reward for my acting my role properly is immediately forthcoming: at the bottom of the drawer I see a notebook with blue covers and a yellow spiral binding. I can always tell which of my notebooks is which by the way they look on the outside. This is the one that I was looking for before, the one that I began the morning of Franco's funeral. I pick it up and sit down opposite him, with my legs crossed, to leaf through it. At my back I can hear the sound of the wind, lashing at the door leading to the terrace. Very Chekhovian — a fireplace would really be just the right touch now.

"May I make a suggestion?" he finally asks, raising his eyes from what he is reading.

I take off my glasses and begin to suck on one of the temple pieces, as I look straight at him. My anxiety on being confronted with his questions has disappeared. We have entered a new phase.

"Why are you looking at me that way? Does it bother you that I've been reading your article?"

"No, I'm waiting to hear your suggestion."

"It's about the book you're thinking of writing."

"I surmised as much."

"I think you ought to take the theme of scarcity as your point of departure. There's a very revealing sentence here."

He lowers his eyes and begins running his finger down the page in search of a line that he's lost. He needs to look at what's written down, otherwise he has no idea where to head from there. I look at my page too. He can say whatever he likes about the theme of scarcity. I have more than enough material to answer him. Finding this notebook was really providential.

I read: "Island of Bergai. First mention of Robinson Crusoe. Dreams of escape." I put my finger on the line to keep my place. I can take off from there. It would make an excellent speech.

"What's the matter? Can't you find it?" I ask him.

"Yes, let's see, you're talking about postwar songs, about how they hadn't yet been turned into consumer items. . . ."

"I remember now."

"Here it is, I'll read what you say: 'In times of scarcity one must make what one has last, and just as no one throws a toy away or leaves a cake half eaten, so it would not occur to anyone to consume a song quickly, because a song is not a luxury that comes one's way every day, but a fundamental item necessary for survival. One takes good care of it, thinks about it, extracts all its juice. . . .'"

"Yes, of course," I interrupt, "exactly as happened to Robinson Crusoe when he arrived on the island. Necessity is the mother of invention."

For the first time he raises his eyes and looks at me, intrigued.

It has been an effective device: when literary or geographical names are not simply bandied about, but are firmly anchored in the concrete history that has made them relevant to the text, they have a very special glow about them. I can see, from the gleam in his eyes, that I have contrived to arouse his curiosity.

"That notebook—where did you dig it up from?" he asks.

I point to the drawer, without further comment. If it seems pertinent, I'll show the notebook to him later, and if not, it doesn't matter.

"Do you talk about Robinson Crusoe in it?"

"Yes, and I also talk about the island of Bergai."

"Bergai? I've never heard that name before."

"That doesn't surprise me. It isn't shown on any map."

One went to Bergai by air. One needed only to look toward the window, conjure up the place with one's eyes closed, and one was transported there by levitation. "Whenever you notice that people don't like you very much," my girlfriend said to me, "or when you don't understand something, come to Bergai. I'll be waiting there for you." It was a secret name. I never mentioned it to a soul, but she's dead now. Even though I remember still that she's flying through the air with me—we've escaped through the window of the Institute— I'm just a little afraid.

"It's an odd name," the man says. "It sounds like an anagram."

"It's a combination of two last names, that of a friend of mine and my own. Telescoping people's first or last names to form the name of most anything was very popular in those days. It's something that's gone almost completely out of style, but in the provinces it was very common: Moga, Doyes, Simu, Quemi. . . ."

"Were they islands too?"

"No, they were shops and cafés that were opened up in those days in Salamanca, modern places."

My father couldn't understand where people got the money to open such places. He used to say that they were the fruit of shady dealings, of black market profits. There was a great deal of talk about what was dirty and what was clean: "That one's hands"—people would say—"aren't as clean as they appear to be." The undermining of values had begun, the waters were becoming muddied, there wasn't any way of making a living that was either completely honest or completely dishonest. Simu was a dark café, with black mirrors and Cubist seats, that had opened up near the Plaza Mayor. My father took my girlfriend and me there one Sunday to have an apéritif. That was the first time in my life I ever saw a girl from a reputable family holding hands with an Italian soldier, in full view of everybody. She took out a cigarette and brazenly began to smoke. She was a blonde who laughed very loudly as she held her glass of vermouth. Everyone stared at her, undoubtedly thinking that her hands weren't as clean as they should be. My father left us alone for a moment and went to congratulate the owner of the place, who was a client of his. We were sitting at a table in the back. More and more people were pouring in. My friend and I smiled, protected by our secret. We began to talk about Bergai. For several months now we'd been jotting down notes about the island in our respective diaries.

"Bergai was invented with exactly that — scarcity — as our point of departure, like all fantasies, like all true affairs of the heart that deserve such a name," I say.

"Affairs of the heart too?"

"Naturally!"

"Are you referring to those that are fed on dreams?"

"Yes, of course."

"Other sorts don't interest you?"

"It's not that they don't interest me, it's that . . ."

"It's that you're afraid of them."

I look away.

"Well, my own case doesn't matter. Everything considered, it would be an isolated example. What's important is to take into account the literary models that shape people's behavior, isn't that so? You need only take a look at world literature. You won't find a single work in which great love affairs were not based on the lack of real satisfactions."

He has lowered his eyes. This would be the moment to launch upon a very brilliant digression on love and absence, illustrated with quotations from the Galician-Portuguese collections of love songs and various Romantic poems. This is a subject on which, after so many years of coming to terms with want and need, I feel I speak with authority. And from there we would go on to romantic novels. This is not a lecture, however, but a performance, where what is called for is improvising in this concrete situation, not embarking upon lifeless artificial discourses. What I would have to do—and I know it, because it frightens me—is to move over to his side and get him to talk to me about the letters that he has stored away in the false-bottomed valise. But I realize that I don't dare take such a step without having first thought of an eloquent phrase, and that, as long as I am searching for this phrase that refuses to come to mind I will not be capable of getting to my feet and crossing, simply and naturally, the few feet that separate us. My failures in love have always stemmed from that, from the fear that someone may leave me at a loss for words, reduced to the naked power of my gaze or my body. "You don't lead them on," my girlfriends used to say to me when I began to go to dances at the Casino. "You don't give them an opening." You had to give men an opening, excite them. Girls who were daring knew how to play the game of give and take, with their eyes, with their laughter, and with the movement of their bodies, even though they had nothing to say. And the men I liked, the ones who perhaps liked me too, took up with some other girl. I learned to turn this defeat into fantasy—it will turn out differently—to dream more fervently, preparing that phrase that I would one day say to a man. I would write a poem, I was in no hurry, and so time went by. "The notary's daughter hasn't gotten herself a serious boyfriend yet, even though she's cute as anything—not pretty, mind you, but cute." Time goes by. I don't dare make the move. I'm missing out on another chance. He's raising his eyes now.

"Tell me about Bergai," he says.

"Well, that means going back to the subject of refuges. You asked me a while ago how old I was when I began to seek out refuges, do you remember?"

"Yes, I remember."

"Well, Bergai was my first refuge. But I invented it with a girlfriend, so I'd have to tell you first about that girlfriend."

I fall silent, how difficult it is to tell all that without talking about the principal miracle, the fact that even though she's dead now, she still keeps flying hand in hand with me. It's rather spooky. I hear the wind blowing violently behind my back. The clothes on the line must be getting whipped to pieces. We're soaring above this terrace. She's wearing a ghost's nightgown and she's laughing. I'm afraid to look back behind me. I begin to talk in confused, disjointed sentences.

"She was the one who got me started writing escape literature. She needed to escape more than I did, because she was worse off than I was. She was in a more helpless position, but at the same time she was more level-headed and more courageous. She faced up to scarcity. The lack of toys for example didn't affect her in the least. She laughed about it, because she had real troubles, do you follow me? Not niggling little ones like mine. She said that a person can invent riches the way Robinson did. We began writing a novel together. Esmeralda scorned riches and ran away from home one stormy night. . . ."

"Your friend's name was Esmeralda?"

"No, she was the heroine of the novel. But I'm telling you all this very badly. The novel was after Bergai. I'm getting lost . . ."

The wind is now close to hurricane force. "Listen, what fun, what a laugh," she shouts in my ear. "He thought I was Esmeralda. And he's Alejandro, right? We've found him, in the flesh." "Don't be so sure, wait and see how all this turns out." "It doesn't matter how it turns out, silly, it's great fun." "Don't shout so, they're going to hear us." "No, they're not, how could they possibly hear us with all this wind? And besides, she's said she's a bit hard of hearing."

"You're getting lost? Well, let's see, go back, we were talking about scarcity . . . a time of scarcity. 'No one left a cake half eaten or threw a toy away,' wasn't that it?"

"Yes, the toy rationing was important. Before the war, my sister and I had lots of fine toys, bought in Madrid, which is where everything that was different came from. Then they stopped buying them for us and we had to begin to "amortize" the investment in the old ones. *Amortize* was a word that everyone used continually. It may be that I had heard it before that without noticing. It was part of my father's legal jargon, which always seemed too abstract to me. But there comes a time when grown-ups' words, however abstract they may be, begin to intrude on your own territory and there's no way to avoid them: that's what happened with *amortize, requisition, ration, hoard, camouflage,* and other similar verbs which were on everyone's lips from morning to night and it was impossible to ignore them. I too used them, even though I had no idea of their exact meaning. But I understood the most important thing, that they had to do with necessity and were the opposite of pleasure. The word *hoard,* for instance, is always associated in my mind with the fable of the grasshopper and the ant. I was once assigned a composition on this subject, a favorite of all the teachers, and I got my revenge by illustrating it with a drawing in which the ant had a huge head and was terribly ugly-looking, whereas the grasshopper was wearing a dress embroidered in gold, like a fairy. I imagined the thrifty ant counting and recounting greasy little well-worn banknotes that didn't even jingle like gold coins and were destined to buy articles of prime necessity. There was a great deal of talk about articles of prime necessity. They took precedence over everything else. They were the opposite of luxury, of the superfluous. Taking a stroll was something superfluous, since it could not be amortized. If we went on an outing in the country, for example, advantage was taken of the occasion to procure lentils, potatoes, or a couple of tender young chickens from some client of my father's, in exchange for a big bundle of those dirty bills. We had no chance to amuse ourselves catching crickets, we had to get back home right away. "We're eating money," my father used to say with a worried expression on his face as we were sitting at the table. That phrase made me lose all my appetite. People thought of nothing but eating, of hoarding things of prime necessity. We soon discovered that toys did not have sufficient merit to be included in this group and that, as a consequence, if after many calculations they bought us one, it had to be amortized. And this law of general amortization eventually applied to the back room as well. . . ."

I break off. I've come to the most important point, I would really have to tell this part well. The man looks at me from the sofa, with his face leaning on his hand. I can't remember at this juncture whether I've mentioned it to him. It's as though I'm in front of a worktable full of file cards that are all mixed up. What's needed is a criterion for putting them in order, organizing them by subject, discarding the repetitions.

"It's impossible. If only you'd brought a tape recorder," I am astonished to hear myself say.

"A tape recorder? Whatever are you saying? How can you possibly be in favor of a gimmick like that?"

"I don't really like them at all, naturally, and furthermore I'm convinced that if you'd brought one with you, I wouldn't be talking to you like this. But I'm surprised that you don't use one. Whenever people come to interview me they always bring one."

"I don't need one. I have another, more subtle apparatus for recording things, and a more dangerous one too."

He looks at me with an ironic expression whose meaning I am unable to make out.

"Do you have it hidden inside your jacket?" I ask jokingly.

"I don't have it hidden anywhere, and it isn't patented yet. It's a system I'm in the process of testing."

I'm glad that I'm sitting with my back to the table. I don't want to turn my head. But it upsets me that he has turned his eyes in that direction again. I can't allow him to go on intruding on my territory.

"Aha! So then you've been using me as a guinea pig!"

"Yes, he answers in a serious tone of voice. "But own up to the fact that you've been using me as one too."

"All right," I interrupt him, "since you seem so sure that you've recorded everything, clear up just one thing for me. Have I already told you about the back room?"

"No, but I presume that must have been a room in your house that was in the back part of it, as its name indicates."

"Yes. Our apartment in Salamanca had two parallel hallways, the one in front and the one in the rear, which were connected by another very small, dark one. There were no rooms off that one, and we called it the bar of the *H*. The rooms on the front hallway overlooked the Plaza de los Bandos, and the ones on the rear hallway—the kitchen, the coal room, the maids' room, the bathroom, and the back room—overlooked an open patio where the laundry basins of the building were. The back room was very large, and in it disorder and freedom reigned. We were allowed to sing at the top of our lungs, move the furniture around as we pleased, jump on top of a rickety old sofa with broken springs that we used to call the poor sofa, to lie on the rug, to get inkstains on it—it was a kingdom where nothing was forbidden. Up until the war, we felt entirely at home there, and there was more than enough room for us to study and play in it. But no one had ever discussed that space with us, nor were there any definite rules governing how it was to be used: the room was ours, period.

"And things changed when the war came along?"

"Yes. There's a sort of dividing line, separating childhood

and adulthood, that began to be marked off in '36. The 'amortization' of the back room and its gradual transformation into a storeroom was one of the first changes that took place on this side of that line."

"It was turned into a storeroom?"

"Yes, but not all of a sudden. First off, I must mention that in the back room there was a large chestnut-wood sideboard. We kept miscellaneous things there, among which an electric plug or a spoon might sometimes turn up, things that someone would come looking for from the other parts of the house. But that did not contravene the principle that that piece of furniture was ours, it was at our entire disposal, it was the cupboard for our junk and our toys, because the purpose of objects is determined by their use, don't you agree?"

"Yes, of course."

"And yet its essential nature as a sideboard constituted the first pretext that was resorted to for the invasion. When the hoarding of articles of prime necessity started, my mother cleared out two shelves and began putting packages of rice, soap, and chocolate on them because she couldn't find room for them in the kitchen. And the conflicts began, first of all over the problem of how to keep in order our various possessions that had been left without a home, and after that the violation of our freedom, since at the most inopportune moment almost anybody might walk in the back room as though he or she owned the place, and on top of that protest if the path to the sideboard wasn't free and clear enough. But up to that point things weren't too bad. The worst began with the partridges."

"Don't tell me you had partridges foisted on you too."

"Yes, stewed partridges. Since there was a great shortage of meat, my mother spent days and days in the kitchen during the hunting season preparing an enormous quantity of stewed partridges, which she then put up in big clay jars with bay leaf and vinegar. There were so many of them that she didn't know where to put them, and naturally they decided that we girls had plenty of space. Those potbellied sarcophagi, lined up against the wall, were the first really bothersome tenants with a sublease on the back room, which up until then had smelled only of erasers and paste. Then after that came strings of sausages hanging from the ceiling, and butter, and so on, until we ceased to have a room to play in because the articles of prime necessity had shoved our childhood aside and driven it into a corner. Play and subsistence cohabited in bitter disharmony, amid incompatible smells."

I pause and glance down at the jottings in the notebook lying open on my knees: "First mention of Robinson, on leaving the china shop on the Calle Corrillo."

"Is there something you've forgotten?" the man asks.

"I've no doubt forgotten so many things. But I'm trying to get to the island. I'm almost there."

"There's no hurry. Defoe took his time to describe in detail the circumstances prior to the shipwreck. They take up at least twenty pages at the beginning of *Robinson Crusoe,* if memory serves me."

"Yes, but I always used to skip those pages."

"I trust you'll grant me that you were wrong to do so."

"Yes, I agree, but at that age the reader is so eager to get on with the story that anything that isn't marvelous seems like mere chaff. It takes one quite a few years to learn to relish the chaff as well."

"There are those who never learn," he says.

I look at him. He's surely thinking of Carola. The two of them are so different. The letters in the trunk struck her as being chaff. This would be a good time to change the subject and talk about the epistolary genre, just to see what would come of it. He appears to be inviting me to do so. There is a strange gleam in his eye. It's my fault that the performance is dragging.

"But just rambling on and on is tiresome too," I say. "Sometimes I envy people who are concise, who always know exactly what to say and exactly where they're heading."

"Don't lie. People like that bore you, as much as they bore me. Would you like a cigarette?"

"Yes."

He puts two of them in his mouth, lights them, and hands me one of them. A touch straight out of a romantic novel. I have to admit that for some time now he has been playing his part much better than I've been playing mine. I half-close my eyes and pause after inhaling the first puff of smoke.

"My sister and I had quite a large toy kitchen, one of the last presents we received before the war, with a little electric stove you plugged in and could really cook things on. We were the envy of all the other little girls. Though as far as playing house was concerned, we had the best time in summer, in the open air, with country children who didn't have store-bought toys and had to use their imagination. They made playthings out of pieces of fruit, stones, and little sticks, and for that very reason they never found their games boring. They would take a flat tile and say 'This is a plate.' They would pound bricks to powder and say 'This is red pepper.' And the whole thing was much more fun, I felt. But when winter came, I forgot and succumbed to the enticements of an industry that encouraged dissatisfaction and the urge to consume. To make a long story short, the equipment in our little electric kitchen had gradually gotten broken, and we were sad because nobody bought us replacements. One afternoon, as I was coming home from the Institute, I saw a marvelous set of porcelain dishes in the window of a china shop — toy dishes, of course, but like real ones, with a gravy boat, dessert plates, and a big fat soup tureen. All the pieces had a design of children riding bicycles, and I wanted the set desperately the moment I laid eyes on it. My father said that it was very expensive, that we'd see when Epiphany came round. But it was the month of March and I was afraid they'd sell it to some other child. It consoled me each time I passed by the window and saw that it was still there, with the price tag on top of it: it cost seven fifty.

"Seven fifty? As little as that?"

"Such a small amount that it's laughable today, seven fifty wouldn't even buy you a bus ride or an ordinary newspaper today, right? But to me it's an important figure. I began to ponder the essential absurdity of money in front of that shop window and those three digits written in red on a piece of cardboard that sometimes tipped to one side or fell over. I would go into the shop to ask if they had lowered the price.

'If we've lowered the price of what?' 'That set of toy china dishes.' I would stand waiting next to the display window as the young clerk went off to ask the shop owner. 'Doña Fuencisla, somebody's asking about that set of toy dishes.' 'The one for seven fifty?' she would answer from the back, a voice impervious to any sort of pleading. 'Yes, ma'am.' 'Well, wrap it up then, you've got paper in there.' I was at a loss as to how to beat a retreat from the shop, or how to cure myself of that vice, till one day I took my friend to see the set — that girl I told you about before. Her opinion seemed vital to me. I had first met her in my class at school only a short time before and I was crazy about her. I saw things through her eyes alone."

"Why? Were you a lesbian?"

Nobody had ever asked me that. If anyone had confronted me with that question at the time I would have answered with another one: "Am I a *what?*" It was a word that was never used, not even secretly. If I had ever heard it, I would have noted it down, just as I did all the others I encountered that were new to me and whose meaning I looked up later in the dictionary. I would surely have regarded what it referred to as unthinkable, something one had to draw a thick veil over, "to pass over quickly like a cat on hot coals," as the Religion teacher used to say when it came time to explain the Sixth Commandment. Expressions such as *fornicate* and *covet thy neighbor's wife* were explained by way of euphemisms that didn't explain anything. Some of the girls found all that beating about the bush very funny. I preferred to ask questions. Allusions to sex scared me, they were impossible to grasp and of ambiguous gender, like butterflies.* "He's a bit of a *mariposo,*" I heard said in my university days of a young man whose mannerisms were very affected. But I did not encounter the words *homosexual* and *lesbian* until years later, in Madrid, and I had considerable difficulty understanding what they meant. I had no place ready in my mind to receive such concepts.

"No," I say, "a thing like that never occurred to me. One can be a lesbian only when one can conceive what is meant by the term, and I'd never even heard that word."

"I asked because you said that you were crazy about your friend."

"What I meant by that was that I admired her endlessly."

"On account of her curly hair?" he asks with a smile.

"No, for two far more unusual things: because she kept a diary and because her parents were in prison. Keeping a diary was a way I could imitate her, and moreover she herself encouraged me to imitate her, but even in my heart of hearts I wouldn't have dared envy her on account of the second thing, however romantic the experience might be, because it seemed to me that God might punish us if I did. An uncle of mine had been executed by a firing squad and my father had not sent us to schools run by nuns and had refused to have Germans billeted in our house. Our parents kept warning us that we shouldn't talk about things like that in public, and sometimes my mother would tell about how it scared her to

---

*The usual word for *butterfly* in Spanish is the feminine *mariposa.* A masculine form of the word, such as *mariposo* or *mariposón,* has the slang meaning of *pansy* or *queer. (Translator's note.)*

wake up in the night on hearing a truck braking abruptly to a stop in front of the house. . . ."

"Go on. What's the matter? You've turned deathly pale."

"I feel frightened all of a sudden, it seems to me there's somebody prowling about there outside."

"It's the wind. A terrible windstorm has come up."

I look at him. I can't allow myself to be afraid as long as he stays here with me. I have to go on telling him stories. If I stop, he'll go away.

"Anyway, my friend began to come over to my house sometimes to study with me, but as for playing together, we only played king-of-the-mountain with the other girls in the courtyard at the Institute. One afternoon, after class, I told her about the set of dishes and asked her to come with me to see it. She didn't say a word and walked on looking straight ahead, with her hands in her pockets, and I was a little annoyed because the enthusiasm with which I described it to her seemed to leave her completely indifferent. She must be waiting to see it for herself, I thought, but when we arrived in front of the shop window and I pointed it out to her, she still didn't show the slightest reaction. She didn't say a word and I didn't dare ask her what she thought. I suddenly felt embarrassed. After we had stood there for a while, she said 'Well, let's go, shall we, it's freezing cold,' and we began to walk toward the Plaza Mayor. That was when she began to talk about Robinson Crusoe. She told me that store-bought toys bored her, that she preferred to play in another way. 'What way is that?' I asked. 'Inventing things. When circumstances are all against a person, the best thing to do is to invent things, the way Robinson did.' I hadn't read that book yet. It had seemed rather boring the times that I'd begun it. I'd never gotten as far as the part about the island, whereas she knew the entire book by heart. We began to walk round and round the Plaza Mayor. She told me in great detail how Robinson had managed to make the best of his bad luck, all the things he had invented to enable him to bear his situation. 'Yes, that's all well and good,' I said. 'But what about us? We don't have an island where we can invent things.' And then she said, 'But we can invent an island together, if you like.' It struck me as a brilliant idea, and so we founded Bergai. That very evening, by the time we separated we had already given it that name, though there were still many details we hadn't gotten around to. But it was very late by then. She was never in a hurry to get home since there was nobody there who would scold her, but I on the other hand was afraid I'd get a good talking-to. 'If they scold you, go to Bergai,' she said. 'It already exists. That's what it's for, a place to take refuge.' And then she also said that it would always exist, even after we were dead, and that nobody could ever take that refuge away from us because it was a secret one. It was the first time in my life that a scolding from my parents didn't upset me. We were having supper and I sat there without turning a hair. I kept looking at them as though I were looking at them from somewhere else, do you understand what I mean?"

"Of course. You were looking at them from the island. You'd discovered how to isolate yourself."

"That's it exactly. The next day, we started making notes about Bergai, each of us in our own diary, with drawings and plans. We kept those notebooks well hidden and didn't show them to anyone except each other. And the island of Bergai began to take shape as a land far removed from our world. It was much more real than the things we saw around us. It had the power and the logical consistency of dreams. I was never again unhappy over toys that got broken, and whenever I was refused permission to do this or that or was reprimanded for something, I took off to Bergai. I could even put up with the fact that the back room was beginning to reek of vinegar without being bothered by it. Everything could be turned into something else, it depended on a person's powers of imagination. My friend had taught me that, she had revealed to me the pleasure of escaping all by oneself, that ability to invent things that makes us feel safe from death."

The man looks at me with eyes filled with emotion. The wind is still howling outside.

"What a marvelous story!" he says. "And what happened to the Bergai diaries?"

"I kept them in the tin chest for some time. After that, I suppose I must have burned them."

"Aren't you sorry you did?"

"Yes, one always idealizes what one has lost, though perhaps I might find them disappointing now. Moreover, if one never lost anything, literature would have no reason for being. Don't you think that's true?"

"Certainly. The important thing is to know how to tell the story of what's been lost, of Bergai, of the letters . . . in that way, they come to life again."

I look him straight in the eye.

"What letters is it you're speaking of?"

He shrugs and averts his eyes.

"I don't know . . . of letters that you've lost. Don't tell me you haven't written love letters at some time or other in your life."

"When have I ever met anyone to write them to? That's a game that depends on another player's appearing and knowing how to spur you on."

"You know that the other player is a pretext."

"Well, pretext or not, he has to exist."

He looks straight at me, with a grave look in his eyes. He says: "You have no need for him to exist. If he doesn't exist, you invent him, and if he does exist, you transform him."

His statement has been too direct and impassioned for us to go back to a conversation that keeps getting bogged down in generalities. I must choose between ignoring the challenge or revealing the secret that I know.

"I really don't know why you say that."

"Well, I don't know either, since I really know you only through what you write. The thing is that I understand literature and know how to read between the lines. I don't think that what I've read tonight has put me off the track: you've spent your life without ever leaving your refuge, dreaming all by yourself. And in the final analysis, you don't need anybody . . ."

"Well! A lot you know!"

"I may be wrong, of course."

"It doesn't matter, go on, even though you may be wrong. . . . Dreaming all by myself . . . of what?"

"Of a great story of love and mystery that you don't dare tell. . . ."

There is a silence. The wind is blowing so hard that it is almost frightening. I lean forward, my eyes seeking his.

"Do you know what my answer is? That I'm not all that sure I dreamed that story," I say slowly, trying to keep my voice from trembling.

His eyes, blank and cruel, gaze into mine.

"Perfect," he says. "But have the courage to tell it, taking precisely that feeling as your point of departure. The feeling that you don't know whether you really experienced what you're recounting or not, that even you yourself don't know. It would be a great novel."

"Ah, I understand now. That's why you said that, in case I want to make it into a novel."

"Why else would I have said it?"

"Of course, why else would you have said it?"

I lower my eyes and bite my lips. I feel an urge to humiliate him, to lay down the secret tricks I hold in my hand and mention Carola, to make a scene like the one she's going to make tonight. But each one of us has an assigned role in life. "Cautious, circumspect literature. Models of conduct characterized by the refusal to take the initiative. Fear of scandal," I read on one of the pages of the notebook.

"Why are you shrugging your shoulders?" he asks me.

"I don't know, it's a gesture I make sometimes," I answer without looking at him.

A tense silence falls. I feel like bursting into tears.

"May I see that notebook?"

"All right, but you won't understand a word. They're just notes."

"Is it the one you began to write on the day of Franco's funeral?"

"The very same one."

"Really? How fortunate, everything is coming to light little by little."

I hold it out to him. I like seeing it in his hands. It's a guarantee. He opens it to the first page.

"'Romantic Rituals in the Postwar Era,'" he reads aloud. "Is that what it's going to be called?"

"That's what occurred to me as a possible title."

"I don't like it at all," he says.

"Well, the title's the least important thing."

"You're wrong there. It affects any number of things."

"And why is it you don't like it?"

"Because it smacks of all your historical research. If that's the title you have in mind, I can see you burying yourself in periodicals libraries again, determined to deal exhaustively with your subject, to make everything absolutely clear. The result would be an estimable piece of work, one strewn with little white pebbles that would be a substitute for the footprints that you yourself have left behind."

"You really have a profound understanding of what literature is all about."

"And so do you," he says. "You've made that clear tonight. And do you know what I'm most grateful to you for?"

I shake my head. A silence follows.

"For allowing me to share the secret of Bergai. It's a secret I'll always keep, I swear to you."

I feel a lump in my throat. It seems as though he is bidding me farewell. We are gazing into each other's eyes, just as we were before the telephone rang. Carola doesn't exist, only he and I.

All of a sudden there is a loud noise behind my back, accompanied by a gust of cold air, and I realize that the door of the terrace has blown open. I stifle a cry, cover in one leap the distance between us, and throw my arms about his neck.

"Who is it, please, please tell me who it is."

I feel his chest pounding mine, his hands on my hair that the wind is ruffling. I close my eyes. I am trembling.

"Come, come, my dear, don't be frightened, it was only the wind. The door blew open in the wind. I'll go close it."

I bury my head in his shoulder. How much I am going to remember in a moment? . . .

"There isn't anybody there outside? Tell me truly. I don't dare look."

"There isn't anybody. Who would there be? Allow me, those sheets of paper you had piled up on the table have been blown all over. And my hat's gone flying through the air with them."

I leave his arms and remain sitting there on the sofa. I see him cross the room, stepping over the scattered pages, and poke his head out the terrace door that is standing wide open. He takes hold of the two leaves of the door to close them, fighting against the wind. It lashes at his black hair, the sheets of paper chase each other about in swirls on the rug and dance around the hat.

"What a hellish night!" he says after he has closed the door.

"By the way, you have some bedsheets hanging on the line out there. They're going to be whipped to pieces."

"It doesn't matter. There wasn't anybody out there, was there?"

"Not a soul. Come and see for yourself if you like."

"No, if you say there wasn't anybody that's good enough for me. Lower the blind though, would you please, and close the curtains?"

"Yes, I was about to do that. But how frightened you were all of a sudden!"

"Yes, I'm trembling, it's stupid of me."

"You're doubtless trembling from the cold as well. Calm down."

He has lowered the blind and drawn the curtains. He now kneels down on the floor, pushes his hat to one side and begins, slowly and deliberately, to gather the scattered pages together, copying my harmonious gestures at the beginning of the scene. It is he who has taken over the reins of the plot again, and my role now is that of a mere extra, trying to control her shivering.

"What a lot of pages!" he exclaims in astonishment. "I didn't think there were that many already written."

"By whom?"

"By you, I presume. May I put them in order?"

"Do whatever you like. And would you kindly hand me that black shawl that's lying over there on the bench in the corner? I'm terribly cold."

He slowly rises to his feet, picks up the shawl, walks over to me, and solicitously drapes it around my shoulders.

"Come, come, my dear, the bad scare you had is over now. Do you know what you ought to do while I put these pages in order? Stretch out on the sofa for a while. Aren't you tired?

"Yes, quite tired."

He helps me put my legs up on the sofa, tucks a cushion under my head. Docilely, voluptuously, I allow myself to be taken care of.

"Relax. Are you comfortable?"

"Oh yes, thank you, very comfortable. You're fine company for me."

He does not answer. One of his hands strokes my forehead for a moment. I close my eyes.

When I open them again, I see him sitting on the floor in front of me, with his back resting against the curtain and the pile of pages on his knees. He is reading them attentively and smiling. A flock of laughing little stars is flying round and round his shoulders and his head in a zigzag pattern. I feel completely at peace.

"I'm getting a bit sleepy," I say. "But don't go."

tHE liᴛᴛlE ɢold box

I FEEL A kiss on my forehead. I open my eyes.

"How did you happen to fall asleep with all your clothes on?"

The light goes on.

A young girl, dressed in jeans and a man's jacket, with a long straight ponytail that's come more or less undone, is sitting at the foot of the big bed, smiling at me.

"I hope you haven't been waiting up for me. I told you not to worry."

She slides the bulky leather bag she's carrying off her shoulder, begins fumbling about inside it and starts taking out various objects that she dumps on top of the bedspread: a memo book, the Leisure Guide, a crumpled pack of cigarettes, two pairs of dark glasses each with a broken lens, her makeup kit, a wristwatch.

"What time is it?" I say automatically.

"Five o'clock," she says, taking a look at the watch.

"That late?"

"Well, you knew I was going to be late. I had to wait for someone to bring me home."

I look toward the window. A hint of milky light is filtering through the curtains. I sit up.

"Don't leave all this stuff strewn on top of the bed. It's heavy."

"It's only for a minute, and then I'll put everything away."

"Whatever are you looking for?"

"Nothing, the 'Respir.' Here it is."

She has taken out a little white plastic tube. She unscrews the cap and puts it to her nose, tipping her head back. She inhales conscientiously.

"So you've caught cold again. It's because you don't bundle up enough."

"It was very nice out tonight when I left, I thought I'd be more than warm enough with my jacket. But anyway, I haven't caught cold, didn't I tell you I was brought home in a car? What a thing you have about getting cold!"

"You came home in a car. From where?"

"From Becerril, of course. I phoned you from there, from Alicia's house, don't you remember?"

"Who drove you home?"

"Juan Pablo."

She starts picking up her things and dumps them back inside her bag. She leaves the pack of cigarettes out and fingers it.

"I'll have just one cigarette here with you and then I'm going off to bed. Do you want one?"

I look at her in surprise and shake my head. She's put her feet up on the bedspread and is leaning her back against the footboard of the bed. Behind her I see the set of shelves lacquered in white, an *étagère* it was called in the years of art deco.

"There's a strange look on your face," she says. "You aren't mad at me by any chance?"

"No. What sort of an evening did you have?"

"Very nice. Do you have any matches?"

I look around. What a mess. I don't see them. The first cigarette I ever smoked was in my second year at the university, at exam time. My friend Mariores gave it to me. She'd learned to inhale. We were at her house, studying dialectology.

"Never mind looking any more, I've just found my lighter."

"I do hope that starting tomorrow you'll put in more time doing some serious studying. It's already the beginning of May."

In the light of the flame that she is now bringing up to her cigarette, I see a look of annoyance cross her face.

"Well, okay, I was already planning to do that, but don't tell me that just as I'm coming home from a party. It's not the right moment."

She's picked up a book that was on top of the bedspread and begins to leaf through it as she smokes in silence.

"Todorov," she says. "How is this book?"

I shrug without saying a word in reply.

"Whatever in the world is the matter with you anyway?"

"Nothing, my head aches."

"It's probably because of the storm. You didn't go out this evening?"

"I don't think so. I don't remember."

"But somebody came to see you, isn't that so?"

I give a sudden start and thrust my feet out of the bed. I lie there motionless with my eyes riveted on the red curtain, and then I look at her.

"Why are you looking at me with such a terrified expression?"

"You said somebody came. . . . What made you say that?"

"Because I saw a tray with two glasses on it out there."

I stand up, as though propelled by a spring, and in two strides cross the space that separates me from the door. I stop on the threshold clutching the curtain with my right hand, and cast a rapid, eager glance all about the space that, from there, is within my view. The room papered in red is empty and silent, like a stage set after the performance is over. I can see, at the far end of it, the black and white tiles of the hallway that leads to the rest of the apartment. A shawl is lying in a heap on the sofa, the drawer of the occasional piece with the mirror appears to be closed, the curtains over the door leading to the terrace are drawn. In front of them, on the floor, is a large, neat pile of sheets of paper, with a paperweight on top, inside which is a miniature Gothic cathedral with iridescent columns. I walk over to that spot, bend down to pick the pile of papers up, and place them on the table. My daughter has come out of the bedroom, I can hear the sound of her breathing behind me. I must hide these pages, nobody must see them. I quickly remove the paperweight and cover them with a large folder.

"Don't worry, I have no intention of snooping. Have you been writing?"

"Yes, a little."

I instinctively pretend to be straightening the other objects lying on the desk. I see the print of Luther and underneath it the blue letter, folded in two.

"That's great! Don't you think so? You've been saying lately that you couldn't manage to get started on anything."

"Well, as you can see, there are attacks of insomnia that get a person somewhere."

"Did you take some Dexedrine?"

I turn around, leaning against the desk, and meet her curious gaze. Before the blue letter appeared, I went to the sewing basket in search of a pill of some sort, yes, perhaps . . .

"I don't remember," I say.

"It doesn't matter, dear, just don't look so worried. I was only asking. What are you thinking about?"

"It's worrying me that I seem to be losing my memory more and more lately, when I used to have such a good one."

"You still do."

"For things in the past, but on the other hand I keep forgetting things I've done just a short while before."

"That's because your mind is somewhere else."

"No, it's because I'm getting old."

"Here we go again. Don't be silly. When I came in a few minutes ago and saw you asleep you looked prettier than ever. You looked like a little girl."

"Really?"

"Really and truly. I was sorry to wake you up, but since you always worry when I come back home in a car and there had been that big windstorm before—you must have heard it, didn't you?"

"I certainly did."

"Up there in the mountains it was awful. That's another reason why I'm so late getting home, we were waiting for it to die down."

I look at the empty sofa with the black shawl lying on it.

"Listen, when you saw me asleep, where was I?"

"What do you mean, where were you? In bed, of course, where else would you have been?"

I go over to the sofa, pick up the shawl, put it around my shoulders.

"The thing is, I lay down here on the sofa and I think I fell asleep here. I don't know when I might have moved to the bed."

"Well, well! That very often happens to me too."

A yawn. Then she walks over to the tray with the thermos and the glasses that is still sitting on top of the little table.

"Well, I'm going to bed. Shall I take this to the kitchen?"

"Do as you like."

"Will you come give me a kiss once I'm in bed?"

"Yes, but I want to finish picking up in here first, and then I'll come right away."

I watch her leave the room with the tray in her hand. All of a sudden, after she's gone out into the hallway, she comes back into the bedroom.

"Hey, what's this darling little box?"

The fleeting vision of her fingers on the little gold box takes my breath away. I turn my eyes toward the right, pretending not to have heard, so as to give myself time to think up some sort of answer. She walks back over to me.

"Your hearing gets worse by the day. I asked you where this little box came from."

"I've had it for a long time. It was a present from a friend."

"I've never seen it before."

"I thought I'd lost it, as a matter of fact, but I found it while I was looking for something else."

"It's adorable. Shall I leave it here for you?"

"Yes, give it to me."

I hear her go off. I stand there holding the little box tightly in the palm of my hand, my ears are buzzing (". . . ever since I left home it was my intention to give it to you"). I close my eyes for a moment. . . . I open them because it seems to me that I have heard a cry of fear. I begin running toward the kitchen and bump into my daughter at the door.

"How horrible, what a giant cockroach! I've never seen such a big one."

"Oh, darling, you scared me, I thought it was something else."

"What did you think it was?"

"How should I know, something much worse. Cockroaches are harmless, my girl."

"That's right, they're harmless, but they scare you too. Don't tell me they don't."

(". . . what terrifies me most is the way they have of appearing just as one is thinking of them. . . .")

"It's run underneath the sink. Please kill it, it was enormous."

"They all look enormous."

I stride resolutely into the kitchen. Another person's fear

helps one to overcome one's own. I have the little gold box in my pants pocket. As I walk over to the sink I give a sigh.

"Go to bed if you like. I'll look for it."

"But don't squash it with your foot. That turns my stomach."

"No, of course not, don't worry. I'll get the spray."

"Okay then, see you in a few minutes. I'll close the door so it doesn't get away. Bring me a glass of water when you come."

I hear the door close behind my back, sounds in the bathroom, footsteps heading down the hallway. I have remained standing there motionless, with no objective, memory, or plan in mind. The space between the mirror and the sideboard has turned into an abandoned game board. There are thousands of holes down which the cockroach might have disappeared, but in order to start searching it out it is necessary to want to play the game, to feel a minimum of excitement or curiosity, and the only thing I feel is drowsiness. I go over to the sink, bend down reluctantly, take out the garbage can. The cockroach isn't there. I sit down for a while on the brown sofa and keep looking at the big closed sideboard, then rest my head on my arms. It's hard for me to imagine that it was once in the back room. Perhaps it was never there. I'm tired.

Finally I get to my feet, open the refrigerator, and fill a glass with cold water. I walk out into the hallway with it. The door to my daughter's room is ajar, I push it open with my foot.

"Here you are, I've brought you your glass of water."

She doesn't answer. She has fallen asleep without turning out the light. I walk across the room on tiptoe, stepping around the books, shoes, and articles of clothing lying on the floor. On the little night table there is not enough uncluttered space to put down so much as a five-duro piece. I push aside a book that is lying face down, Dashiell Hammett's *The Thin Man:* ". . . contradictory clues, false trails, a surprise at the end," I read on the back jacket. I leave the glass there for her, bend over to give her a kiss, and she stirs slightly, smiling with her eyes closed.

I am again in bed with blue pajamas on and one elbow leaning on the pillow. The place formerly occupied by Todorov's book is now occupied by a pile of numbered pages, one hundred eighty-two of them. On the first one is written, in capital letters with a black ballpoint pen: THE BACK ROOM. I pick it up and begin to read:

". . . And yet I'd swear that the position was the same. I think I've always slept this way, with my right arm underneath the pillow and my body turned slightly over onto that side, my feet searching for the place where the sheet is tucked in . . ."

How sleepy I'm getting! I take off my glasses, put the pages aside, and lay them carefully on the floor. I stretch my legs out till they touch the place where the sheet is tucked in, and as I put my right arm underneath the pillow, my fingers encounter a small, cold object. I close my eyes with a smile and clasp it in my hand. As the laughing stars begin to rush by, I have recognized it by the feel of it: it is the little gold box.

Madrid, November 1975 – April 1978